SMARTPOOP 1.0

THIS AI WENT WHERE NO HUMAN WILL EVER GO

WRITTEN BY

LÊ NGUYÊN HOANG

AND

TRISTAN LE MAGOAROU

2021

Contents

SmartPoop 1.0

This AI went where no human will ever go

Welcome to *SmartPoop 1.0*, a novel written by Lê Nguyên Hoang and Tristan Le Magoarou, published under licence CC BY 4.0 (freely reusable with attributions to the authors).

The book is available on GitHub, in epub and in pdf.

The book is currently in beta test.

Outline

Why this book?

SmartPoop 1.0 aims to be a very realist science fiction, whose goal is to raise awareness of the danger of algorithms and the challenges to make them robustly beneficial.

It tells the story of a tech start-up, *SmartPoop*, which produces automated poop analysis. This allows for highly personalized medical diagnosis. However, in each chapter, the deployment of *SmartPoop* leads to *unwanted side effects,* whose medical and social consequences are usually tragic. The co-founders of *SmartPoop*, who are the main characters, must then take the responsibility of their technology, accept the consequences, and find solutions to make their products more secure and ethical.

About the authors

Lê Nguyên Hoang

Lê Nguyên Hoang is a science researcher and communicator of the School of Computer and Communication Sciences at EPFL, in Switzerland. His research focuses on the security and safety of algorithms, especially on the theory of learning and on their collaborative design. Lê is also a YouTuber, on his channels Science4All (English), Wandida, EPFL and ZettaBytes, EPFL. He wrote three books, *The Equation of Knowledge*, *Le fabuleux chantier* et *Turing à la plage*. He is also a member of the ethics counsil of the French telecommunication company Orange. Finally, Lê is Président of the Tournesol Association, whose platforme aims to collect a large, reliable and secure database of ethical human judgments, to help solve the ethics of algorithms.

Tristan Le Magoarou

Doctor of Medicine, specialist in public health and social medicine, Tristan Le Magoarou is a medical information and public health doctor in a provincial hospital center. He is also, since 2016, a YouTuber on his channel Risque Alpha which has 27,000 subscribers where he popularizes epidemiology and statistics.

Autres

The illustration of the book was made by Thibault Roy. The book also results from many interactions with a large number of people to which the authors are indebted, including El Mahdi El Mhamdi, Mariame Tighanimine, Sébastien Rouault, Ly An Hoang, Aidan Jungo, Alexandre Maurer, Sylvain Hippolyte, Felix Grimberg and Oscar Villemaud, among others.

About the writing of the book

This book will be constantly updated to make it more readable, more credible and more relevant. We invite our readers in particular to suggest corrections, whether typographical or in terms of the story. Note however that the authors

Lê Nguyên Hoang and Tristan Le Magoarou will have the final say on the version available on this github, and that they work on it as volunteers. Note that the CC BY 4.0 license allows anyone to reuse and adapt the book as they wish, as long as they credit the original version of the book and its authors. We encourage such efforts, and are available for any such project.

9

1. The brown gold

After he opened a bottle of champagne and filled the glasses, Marc Rofstein asks for the attention of the five guests of the evening organized by Katia Crapinski, in their flat.

> Dear friends, I would like us to take a few moments to solemnly congratulate Katia. Her latest research paper has been accepted for publication[1], which means that Katia now has everything she needs to write and validate her PhD thesis in machine learning[2]. So, with this great news in mind, I'd like to invite you to raise your glasses, and celebrate the soon-to-be-Doctor Crapinski for her accomplishments - even if, unlike me, Katia won't be a life-saving doctor. Here's to soon-to-be Dr. Crapinski!

Later that evening, after feigning appreciation for her roommate's joke, Katia shares her desire to do work that is more altruistic and beneficial to all humanity. Her research so far is limited to improving the performance of already existing algorithms[3]. However, Katia is well aware that these advances mainly feed the

---

[1] Scientific production relies heavily on a system of publication in scientific journals or conferences, where acceptance for publication depends on peer review. A submitted article is thereby analyzed by two to five reviewers, each of whom issues an opinion, and demands more or less major corrections. Scientific journals and conferences vary greatly according to their preferred topics and their prestige. In computer science, publications in scientific conferences are very prestigious. In machine learning in particular, the most prestigious conferences are NeurIPS, ICML, and ICLR, with conferences like COLT, AISTAT, UAI, and AAAI, among others, close behind.
Video. The Peer Review Process. American Chemical Society (2019).

[2] A thesis in computer science is usually a collection of papers accepted for publication. The thesis author is usually required to add an abstract, a general introduction, and a conclusion. Depending on the university, the requirements to have a thesis accepted vary.

[3] Many thinkers consider that, while technological progress greatly improves the quality of life of most, it also drastically decreases the cost of causing a monumental catastrophe. If one accepts this postulate, any research on the performance of algorithms can be seen as the potential creation of new and poorly controlled risks, and is therefore dangerous. To characterize this phenomenon, the philosopher Nick Bostrom speaks of "the vulnerable world hypothesis". He proposes a metaphor where scientific research consists in drawing a ball from an urn, containing white and black balls. Each white ball improves the world. But to draw

recommendation of addictive content by social medias[4] and the optimization of targeted advertising on these platforms[5]. Can't this same technology be used to rather save lives and make the world actually better?

Marc, still a student in oncology, suggests the use of algorithms for early diagnosis. A cancer diagnosed early is more likely to be treated successfully, and with fewer risks and complications.

> It's starting to happen, says Marc. Last year, American researchers showed that an AI was as good as a team of dermatologists at detecting skin cancers on photos[6]. But unfortunately, in this year 2018, many cancers are still diagnosed late. At this stage, risky and expensive care is needed.

> There is clearly a need for learning algorithms in medicine. But if

---

a black ball is to put it in grave danger, like the discovery of the nuclear chain reaction. According to Bostrom, the blind quest for new knowledge would thus pose an existential risk, and would therefore be immoral. This seems to be all the more the case when it comes to the quest for more efficient algorithms, whose rushed deployment at scale certainly has side effects that are difficult to foresee. Given this, it seems urgent to guide the research towards the search for "white balls", rather than letting it blindly draw any sort of balls. Better yet, research investments could be rather directed towards the search for white balls that protect us from black balls that could be drawn in the future. In the context of computer science, this would typically correspond to funding vastly more research on AI ethics and security, rather than on AI performance (and, say, valuing more the former kind of research in peer review and when citing others' research).
How civilization could destroy itself – and 4 ways we could prevent it | Nick Bostrom. TED (2020).
The Vulnerable World Hypothesis. Nick Bostrom. Global Policy (2019).

[4]These days, the most sophisticated "artificial intelligences", the ones that receive billions of dollars of investment in research and development per year (if not a lot more still!), are indeed the algorithms of the web, because the economic stakes and the need for automation are monumental there. After all, the turnover of Google, Apple, Facebook, Amazon and Microsoft, among others, can be counted in hundreds of billions of euros. Any service improvement of a few percent therefore represents billions of euros. But these companies have to manage billions of users' data, and each user may generate megabytes of data per week. For example, in 2013, Facebook received 350 million new photos every day, or one photo for every ten users. For 3-megabyte photos, that's an average of 2 megabytes of photos uploaded per user per week. **Journal.** Facebook Users Are Uploading 350 Million New Photos Each Day. Business Insider (2013) As another example, in 2019, every hour, there are 30,000 hours of new videos uploaded to YouTube. Such enormous amounts of data can only be processed by machines. Unfortunately, the machines' tasks are increasingly complex, such as detecting hate speech in an image or identifying misinformation in billions of posts.
Web. YouTube's Blog.

[5]As a *mea culpa*, Lê Nguyên Hoang, one of the authors of this book, acknowledges that, back in 2015, his academic research tackled mathematical problems whose primary application was the optimization of such ads. He now believes that this work was in fact unethical, as this novel will later illustrate. Since then, he completely reoriented his research towards AI ethics and safety.

[6]**Paper.** Dermatologist-level classification of skin cancer with deep neural networks. Andre Esteva, Brett Kuprel, Roberto A. Novoa, Justin Ko, Susan M. Swetter, Helen M. Blau & Sebastian Thrun. Nature (2017).

we want to diagnose anything, we need data. Lots of data[7], Katia
points out.

Unfortunately, simply collecting data is a laborious, delicate and intrusive task
for the general public, who would rather not worry about cancer risks.

> We can't even get people to cut down on smoking or drinking, notes
> Marc. If you want to have any chance of making early diagnoses,
> you have to focus on very informative data. But that kind of data
> is usually too invasive to collect. I don't know many people who
> volunteer to have their blood drawn[8] repeatedly, for example...

Katia looks thoughtful. How could she acquire patient data? Or, better yet,
how could she acquire data from non-patients? And how could it be done
without being "invasive"? Katia also wonders who came up with the term
"invasive". A blood test rarely "invades" people's bodies.

It is with these thoughts in mind that Katia heads for the bathroom to relieve
herself.

Eureka

As she sits on the bowl, Katia suddenly raises her head. Her thoughtful face
suddenly turns into a radiant smile. Like Archimedes[9], Katia rushes of the
bathroom, and gives a speech that will change her destiny, as well as all of
humanity's.

> Marc, I have just found the idea of the century. I know how to
> solve this diagnostic problem! You said it. We need data. A lot of

---

[7] The data issue is really critical in machine learning, since algorithms are systematically designed to learn from data and generalize from data.

[8] Founded in 2003 by Elizabeth Holmes, the company Theranos has long claimed to provide a general health checkup from a minimal blood sample. In 2015, Theranos was valued at \$9 billion. But in 2018, Theranos was sued for "massive fraud." Theranos' supposedly revolutionary technology never actually worked. Theranos employees appear to have been covertly exploiting conventional blood testing techniques, the reliability of which was in fact questionable.

Video. Elizabeth Holmes exposed: the \$9 billion medical 'miracle' that never existed. 60 Minutes Australia (2021).

[9] According to legend, to determine whether a crown was really made of gold, Archimedes had the idea of measuring its volume, by measuring the amount of water displaced in a full bathtub when the crown was placed in the tub. By combining this measurement with the measurement of the mass of the crown, Archimedes could then estimate whether the crown had the density of a gold crown. When he realized this, according to legend, Archimedes was in the bathtub. He exclaimed "Eureka", and went out naked in the street to share the enthusiasm of his discovery.

data that is very informative, but also very simple to collect. Data that we won't need to violently extract from human bodies; because these data come out naturally from human bodies. These data have gone through the whole human body, and contain in them all kinds of traces of the state of this body[10]. These data, today, we throw them away every time we flush. But imagine what we could diagnose if, instead of flushing them down the drain[11], we carefully collected this data and took the time to analyze it! Marc, we need to analyze pee and poo!

In the days that follow, Katia and Marc spend their time discussing this feces testing project. They conclude that the ideal product would be a smart toilet[12], capable in particular of measuring and analyzing an excrement in all its aspects before its journey in the wastewater. However, such a product would require years of research and development, and therefore a large number of investors. As a starter, the two friends are leaning towards a less ambitious project. After all, as Katia points out, the best modern information gathering tool is the telephone. Why not use it to take poop pics?

Thus was SmartPoop born, with the intent to be an application for collecting photographic samples of fecal matter and for the automated analysis of these images using machine learning algorithms. During the following months, Katia writes her PhD thesis during the day, and programs SmartPoop until late at night.

During this time, Marc learns about coprology. He downloads public databases of excreta, and takes care to check their labels[13]. Some feces are small solid balls; a clear indication of constipation. Others are an almost liquid mush; a classical diarrhea. Some turds have a perfectly wavy shape; a sign of very good intestinal health[14]! The color also gives information about liver function or the

---

[10] Archaeologists are particularly fond of fossilized poop, which allows them to learn about the diet and health of past populations.
Video. Viking Poo is One of the York's Biggest Archaeological Discoveries? Channel 4 Documentaries (2020).

[11] Actually, it is still possible to make medical diagnoses from sewage analysis. In fact, this was done in the COVID-19 epidemiological follow-up. The concentration of Sars-CoV-2 RNA in sewage allows to infer the incidence of the virus in a sometimes very localized population.
Paper. How sewage could reveal true scale of coronavirus outbreak. Smriti Mallapaty. Nature (2020).

[12] Smart toilet projects really exist! In fact, there is a publication in the scientific journal *Nature Biomedical Engineering* about a prototype, capable of doing anal recognition!
Paper. A mountable toilet system for personalized health monitoring via the analysis of excreta. Seung-min Park et al. Nature Biomedical Engineering (2020).

[13] Data *labeling* is a critical phase in the design of training databases for learning algorithms. It consists of taking raw data (such as images), and annotating the image with relevant information, such as the presence or absence of cats, or such as the health status of the person who produced the photographed excrement.

[14] **Video.** MinuteEarth Explains: Poop. MinuteEarth (2020).
Book. Gut: The Inside Story of Our Body's Most Underrated Organ (Revised Edition). Giulia Enders. Greystone Brooks (2018).

presence of blood.

> You know, in fact, stools should be colorless or whitish, Marc explains to Katia during one of their work evenings. It's mostly water and fiber after all. But it's a waste product of red blood cells, bilirubin, that makes it dark. It's the liver that processes it and "puts it" in the feces.

> I see... and so when the liver doesn't work, poop turns brown?

> Almost. Yellow rather. That's what we call jaundice. Or "jaundice" if you prefer, and the stools become whitish. But you see...

Katia was already no longer listening, thinking about what kind of color analysis she could integrate into their algorithms. "SmartPoop is going to be so cool[15]", she said to herself.

The app is live!

In March 2019, Katia defends her thesis. One week later, the SmartPoop application is made available on the Apple Store and the Google Play Store[16]. In its initial version, SmartPoop thus allows users to create a database of their solid droppings, which Marc spends each evening analyzing.

> I spent some boring evenings during my medical school years, seeing some pretty nasty stuff... but those were almost the worst, Marc would later say.

SmartPoop also has learning features[17]. In particular, it learns progressively from the data, daily labeled by Marc, and then generalizes Marc's labels to

---

[15]The word "cool" is often used to describe certain "newsworthy" technologies. There is certainly some important thinking to be done around what makes a technology or idea "cool." In particular, this may sometimes not be directly related to the ability of the technology or idea to actually make the world better. Typically, many technologists seem to find decentralized cryptocurrencies or the performance of machine learning algorithms "cool." However, it seems that this can sometimes lead them to ignore or underestimate the dangers of these technologies.

[16]A quick search on Google Play Store reveals that there are already many apps for tracking feces, such as Poop Tracker (4.5 stars, 100k+ downloads)., PoopLog (4.2 stars, 100k+ downloads). and Poopify (4.6 stars, 10k+ downloads)..

[17]The most widespreaf form of machine learning is what is called *supervised learning*. This is the problem of guessing properties (called *labels*) of raw data like images. Typically, images with a cat can be labeled with the label "cat". In the case of SmartPoop, images of constipation will be labeled "constipation". The learning algorithm will then try to identify features that the "constipation" images have, and that the non-constipation images do not have. If the algorithm is successful, it will then exploit these features to then generalize the "constipation"

predict the risk of constipation or diarrhea in users from images that Marc has not had the time to view[18].

Katia spends her days improving her application by night, and promoting SmartPoop by day. She is particularly active in research institutes, hospitals and homes for the elderly, but also in entrepreneurial networks like Station F in Paris. Her TEDx at the London School of Economics earned her a standing ovation from an audience won over by the health opportunity.

However, after months of promotions, SmartPoop did not take off. If the application is downloaded 1587 times, it is only used daily by 75 users[19] (including about twenty among Katia and Marc's relatives). In July 2019, four months after the application went online, Katia realizes that SmartPoop is a failure.

> SmartPoop would become a must-have if we had a lot more data to train more sophisticated algorithms to predict rarer and more dangerous diseases. The health potential is still huge, she tells Marc. But we greatly overestimated the motivation of users to support such a public health project[20]... With hindsight, I would say that we were far too nice and naive in our project management. The venture capitalists were right. We should have thought much more about growth, user acquisition and marketing the product. We might have realized earlier that SmartPoop is a waste of time. Even if we continue our promotional work for years, we may never exceed 1000 regular users. And that won't be enough to acquire enough data to have a useful diagnostic tool. SmartPoop is hopeless.

Frustrated, Katia gives up SmartPoop, and accepts a job as a computer developer in a large company, which she started in September. However, in spite of the exceptional work environment offered to her, Katia is not particularly enthusiastic about her job. But at least, she thinks, it allows her to pay her rent.

---

label to non-labeled images that have the features of "constipation" images.

Much of the design of supervised learning machine learning algorithms is then played out in the annotation of the data. In fact, this work is so laborious that web companies often take advantage of the users of their platforms to do this work for them, typically via "CAPTCHAs" that also verify that the user is human.

[18]One of the great advantages of algorithms over humans is what is called their ability to *scale*. So if an algorithm has the same diagnostic performance as a human from images, it can be used relatively cheaply by billions of users at the same time. This offers fantastic commercial opportunities, but also medical or philanthropic ones. As an example, thanks to new information technologies, the GiveDirectly association allows anyone to give money directly to poor people in disadvantaged countries, without going through intermediaries who could keep the money for themselves and with almost no intermediate cost. Web. GiveDirectly.

[19]The big challenge of many web products is often user retention.

[20]Other more playful initiatives are already commercially successful, such as the Foodvisor which estimates the calories in a meal from a photo.

The ROVID-19

At the end of November 2019, however, an event will change the future of humanity in general, and that of Katia in particular. Kormica[21] declares a worrying multiplication of a new, highly contagious and potentially deadly pathology, which seems to affect thousands of Kormicans, and which seems to have already claimed hundreds of victims. The following month, in December 2019, similar cases are observed in Bokistan[22], and soon enough, in more and more countries around the world. The World Health Organization declares a state of emergency: a new pandemic is on its way.

A few months later, the culprit is found. It's a new rotavirus. The terrible disease it causes is named "ROtaVIrus Disease 2019", or ROVID-19[23]. ROVID-19 causes many disturbing symptoms, such as stomach aches, headaches, increased fatigue, heavy diarrhea, high fevers, vomiting, and tremors, which lead nearly 10% of those infected to death. This terrible disease seems to be particularly deadly in young people under 30.

But what makes ROVID-19 extremely dangerous is its extreme contagiousness. Worse still, the tracing of infections shows that this contagiousness is particularly high two or three days before the first symptoms appear. This is called *pre-symptomatic* infection. Infected persons are not yet aware that they are ill when they transmit the disease to others. The basic reproduction number[24] of the virus, i.e. the average number of individuals that an infected person will infect, is estimated to be about 8. The exponential[25] growth of the pandemic is rapidly terrifying every health agency, hospital and government in the world.

---

[21] In October 2021, Google Translate translated "poop" into "korm" in Ukrainian. However, it turns out that korm means "animal food", not "poop".

[22] "Bok" means "poop" in Turkish.

[23] ROVID-19 is, of course, a fictional disease inspired from COVID-19, which struck the world in November-December 2019.

[24] The basic reproduction number is the average number of individuals that an infected person will infect, absent interventions to control the spread of an epidemic. It is estimated that COVID-19 initially had a basic reproduction number of about 3, and that the Delta variant has a much higher rate (but difficult to estimate, since it appeared at a time when many interventions were already in place). This is an important quantity because, if it is greater than 1, then the epidemic will spread exponentially in the absence of intervention.
The effective reproduction rate is the average number of individuals that an infected person will infect, knowing all the sanitary measures in place. This is ultimately the most important variable. If it is greater than 1, then the epidemic will spread exponentially. If it is less than 1, then the epidemic will disappear exponentially fast. In practice, due to lax sanitary measures, especially in the case of COVID-19, this rate fluctuates around 1, making the epidemic an *endemic*, i.e. a disease that persists in the general population.
Blog. What Happens Next? COVID-19 Futures, Explained With Playable Simulations. Marcel Salathé & Nicky Case (2020).
Video. Epidemic, Endemic, and Eradication Simulations. Primer (2020).

[25] Exponential growth occurs when the number of cases is multiplied each week by a constant greater than 1. The danger of such growth is that it seems insignificant in the first few weeks, but suddenly gets out of control after a few weeks or months.
Video. Exponential growth and epidemics. 3Blue1Brown (2020).

In early January 2020, all countries across the globe are entering lockdown periods in turn, as medical tests are slowly being put in place[26], including group tests[27]. January's estimates are terrifying. Hundreds of thousands of people around the world appear to be already affected, and tens of thousands of victims have already died.

An initial suspicion is slowly gaining momentum in the scientific community, particularly following the observation of a meteoric rise in cases among wastewater treatment technicians. A growing body of evidence, including chemical analyses of patients' feces, suggests that the ROVID-19 virus is spread primarily via the flatulence of infected individuals.

"A very nice study by a team from Toulouse also showed large clusters of sick people among people who often frequented restaurants specializing in cassoulet[28]," Marc often said to lighten the anxious atmosphere that prevailed at the time. The wearing of filtering diapers[29] was then advised for all people who needed to move around, to avoid transmitting the virus.

The quest for data

What if SmartPoop could help? This is a question Marc asks Katia shortly after the lockdown begins. Katia responds that she is unfortunately exhausted and overwhelmed by the migration of many of her company's products to remote-friendly solutions. But while Katia is still working out bugs in her code at 11pm, Marc insists.

> We know that the ROVID-19 virus is not only very present, but also very active in the stool. It is most certainly the way it spreads the

---

[26] It is always good to remember that a medical test does not certify whether or not a person has the disease in question, because tests are always imperfect. In fact, if an individual receives a positive (imperfect) test for an extremely rare disease, then it is generally still likely that he or she is not in fact ill (other symptoms should be analyzed). The mathematics of conditional probabilities is critical to the proper interpretation of these medical tests.
Video. The medical test paradox, and redesigning Bayes' rule. 3Blue1Brown (2020).

[27] In a group tests, samples from, say, 10 subjects are mixed and tested all at once. This way, if the group test is negative, which will often be the case for rare diseases, then all 10 subjects can be cleared at once. Otherwise, the subjects can be tested individually.
Paper. Group testing against Covid-19 Christan Oliver & Olivier Gossner. EconPol Policy (2020).
Book. Combinatorial group testing and its applications. Ding-Zhu Du & Frank Hwang. World Scientific Publishing Company (1999).

[28] "Cassoulet" is a French delicacy, which is made of a lot of white beans. Yet white beans are known to provoke larger amounts of intestinal gas production.
Paper. Gas production in humans ingesting a soybean flour derived from beans naturally low in oligosaccharides. Fabrizis Suarez, John Springfield, Julie Furne, Troy Lohrmann, Philipp Kerr & Michael Levitt. The American Journal of Clinical Nutrition (1999).

[29] The contagiousness of the fart, but also the ability of clothing to filter farts, was tested and verified by Dr. Karl Kruszelnicki, following an experiment with farts in Petri dishes. "Our final conclusion? Don't fart naked near food."
Paper. Hot air? Michael Doyle. The Canberra Times, Reprinted on BMJ (2021).

most. But that also means that it must be leaving traces in the stool. Today, we can detect these traces by looking directly for bits of RNA of the virus with classical biology methods[30]. But if the virus is so present, it is possible that it leaves a visible trace in the stool; that it makes the stool visually different. I've seen some pictures of contaminated material, and unfortunately, I couldn't spot any meaningful difference. But if there is even a small difference, maybe an algorithm will be able to see it. And if so, we could isolate the ROVID-19 cases, and perhaps control the pandemic without lockdown. That would save millions of lives, perhaps hundreds of millions of lives. Not to mention all the mental health problems...

Katia then makes the connection to a call for proposals she saw going around at work, which was actively looking for ROVID-19-related programming projects. Surely, she thought, investors would be interested in a project like SmartPoop, if SmartPoop promises to solve the ROVID-19 crisis. But to convince them, you'll first need to have a *Proof of Concept*, or PoC as we say in the jargon[31]. In other words, it will be necessary to have a first version of SmartPoop, not quite functional yet, but convincing enough to attract these investors. But for that, Katia knows that SmartPoop is mostly missing data.

We need data from sick patients. A lot of data from a lot of sick patients, exclaims Katia. Do you think you can get us that?

Marc then spends his days contacting every colleague in his address book, then every doctor he knows on Facebook, then every doctor he finds on Twitter, begging them to take pictures of patients' feces in hospitals. Most don't respond[32]. Some retort with insults. "Have you ever been in a hospital? We're already overworked to save lives. We're not here to feed a crappy Instagram account," the most aggressive doctors reply. "They abuse... We can't put any filters on, and you can't make a story out of it," Marc quips.

---

[30]The most standard method for detecting bits of RNA is the qPCR test. It consists of replicating a piece of target RNA a large number of times, via a polymerase chain reaction, and inserting a fluorescent signal into the copies. This allows to exponentially increase the number of these RNA pieces, if they were initially present in the analyzed sample, which makes them easier to detect later.
Video. PCR - Polymerase Chain Reaction Simplified. MEDSimplified (2019).

[31]In innovation, and especially in IT, the design of a new product usually starts with the PoC, which allows to attract investments, in time and money, to then develop a functional product. The second step is then the design of a *Minimum Viable Product*, or MVP. This product is meant to be minimalist (to be manufactured quickly), but perfectly functional (to be sold to the first customers). New features can then be added to the MVP.

[32]The issue of hospital data is actually horribly more complex, not least because of considerations for protecting sensitive patient data. Indeed, hospital IT infrastructure is often subject to attack by malicious hackers, who often exploit the lack of investment in the security of that infrastructure to cripple services and demand ransom. In the context of the novel, however, one can imagine that the health situation may be dire enough to (ethically) justify (illegal) collaborations with SmartPoop.

Katia then adapts the SmartPoop.com website to call on doctors, but also the general public to contribute. She asks visitors to use SmartPoop to take pictures of their excrements, and to inform on the platform their health status day after day. She also implores doctors to encourage their patients to use SmartPoop.

Katia is also contacting science communicators on Twitter and YouTube to promote the project. Science4Alpha[33], a science YouTuber with 200,000 subscribers, agrees to popularize Katia's project. The very educational video of Science4Alpha collects 100,000 views in the first week, and leads to the adoption of SmartPoop by tens of thousands of users[34].

In May 2020, as case numbers slowly decline but still remain very high, SmartPoop is harvesting hundreds of thousands of photographs daily. In total, SmartPoop then has tens of millions of photos of feces. Unfortunately, while Katia's algorithms easily distinguish glowing diarrhea from advanced cases, they still fail to detect any difference between pre-symptomatic[35] infected cases and healthy cases. Katia is frustrated.

It seems like a waste of time, she exasperated to Marc.

Are you still regretting our efforts?

No... I think this time the bet was right[36]. There was little chance

---

[33] The name Science4Alpha is a nod to the Science4All and Risk Alpha channels of the two authors of this novel.

[34] "Without our science communicators to publicly inform, explain, teach, decode, counter misinformation and debate science matters many would remain in a space where they don't have [the] information they need, leading to poor choices being made at really crucial times," said Jacinda Arden, Prime Minister of New Zealand, in July 2020. Unfortunately, collaborations between institutions and science communicators, during the COVID-19 crisis and around topics such as climate change or the ethics of algorithms, have arguably been very deficient around the world. More generally, there is arguably a more general lack of investment in science communication. Such collaborations are also often very delicate, for both instiutions and science communicators, especially in the current climate of mistrust. For example, Science4All's video on vaccines, in collaboration with the French Ministry of Health, caused an uproar (probably accentuated by an organized disinformation campaign), receiving more dislikes than likes on YouTube (which is extremely rare!).
Video. Un vaccin pour permettre aux étudiants de retrouver leur vie d'avant (ft. Prof. Fischer). Science4All (2021).

[35] In the case of COVID-19 (and therefore ROVID-19), the great challenge of pandemic control was precisely the avoidance of pre-symptomatic infections, i.e. by infected individuals before they develop symptoms (and therefore before they realize they are infected).
Paper. Evidence for pre-symptomatic transmission of coronavirus disease 2019 (COVID-19) in China. Ren et al. Influenza (2020).

[36] Katia insists on the difference between the *bet* and the result. As the former poker player Annie Duke explains, we humans are unfortunately too prone to judge a decision by its outcome, even if that outcome was unpredictable at the time of the decision, especially given the information available at the time. In order to make progress, according to Duke, it is critical to judge the decision made on the basis of the state of knowledge at the time the decision was made, which was then necessarily a gamble, because the future was uncertain.
Book. Thinking in Bets: Making Smarter Decisions When You Don't Have All the Facts. Penguin. Annie Duke (2019).

that SmartPoop would solve the ROVID-19 crisis. But if it did, we would have saved humanity. Well, we didn't. But, this time, I think we did the right thing by trying. But it's still frustrating...

Disappointed, Marc acknowledges that the lockdowns are likely to drag on, probably for years, until an effective vaccine is developed, tested and deployed on a very large scale - if it ever sees the light of day[37]. Meanwhile, ROVID-19 will continue to spread.

Upon hearing these words, Katia stands up, waving her right index finger, which then illustrates the intellectual bubbling that animates her neurons.

To spread... But yes! This is it!

Katia then throws herself on her computer, and starts to code. Marc follows her and asks for explanations. What is Katia's new idea ?

SmartPoop versus ROVID-19

The ROVID-19 virus spreads particularly well through flatulence, Katia explains. But from what I understand, flatulence doesn't usually spread very far, because we wear panties and pants. Well also skirts and dresses... But forget about skirts and dresses. They have been forbidden for months now! For ROVID-19 to spread really well, it probably has to affect the way gases are produced and diffused. But that gas, it must also be present in the feces! And we should see it. But not in a picture. To see it, you need a video!

That's why SmartPoop proposes from now on, not to photograph the excrements, but to film them. A few days later, hundreds of thousands of videos of a few seconds are collected by SmartPoop. Katia, who has not slept in the meantime, is about to complete the design of SmartPoop's new algorithms, now adapted to video analysis.

At 4 a.m., Katia goes into Marc's room to wake him up. "I finished the algorithm. You need to see this". Marc wakes up with a start, runs to get a bottle of champagne and joins Katia in the living room. Katia explains that she has trained her algorithm with 90% of SmartPoop's database, and that she is about

---

[37]It's worth remembering that at the beginning of the COVID-19 pandemic, it wasn't clear that the vaccines would be as effective as they eventually were. And it's also worth remembering that some vaccines have been successful in eradicating some terrible diseases, like smallpox.
Video. How we conquered the deadly smallpox virus - Simona Zompi. TED-Ed (2013).

to test the algorithm's performance on the remaining 10%[38]. Katia explains that these remaining 10% were drawn at random, with the simple constraint that they contain as many infected pre-symptomatic feces as healthy feces[39]. If the algorithm fails, then it will have a 50% excreta recognition rate. If it is perfect, its accuracy will be 100%.

All that remains is to run the algorithm's test to see how it performs. Katia and Marc launch into a countdown. Five. Four. Three. Two. One. The test is launched[40].

Ten seconds later, 10% of the test is done. You will have to wait another minute and a half to get the results. During this long minute and a half, Katia and Marc are breathless. Finally, the result is displayed. The verdict: 52.4%.

Head down, Marc gets up and goes to put the champagne back in the fridge. Katia slumps into the sofa. When Marc returned to the living room, Katia was already asleep. He goes to seek a cover for her to avoid taking cold to her. Then he goes to bed in his turn. The following day, Marc wakes up at 3 pm. Katia is still sleeping. In fact, Katia will have slept twenty hours in a row.

SmartPoop's rise

It is still in the middle of the night that Katia suddenly wakes up Marc.

> Five standard deviations, five standard deviations[41], she repeats! The test did not fail. It is in fact quite clearly above 50%.

---

[38] What is described here is the separation of the dataset into a *training set* and a *test set*, which is a classical technique in machine learning to validate an algorithm after learning. Sometimes, an intermediary *validation set* is used to anticipate overfitting risks before running the trained algorithm on the *test set*.
Video. Train, Test, & Validation Sets explained. deeplizard (2017).

[39] Note that the prediction success rate of an algorithm is highly dependent on the rate of things to be detected in the data (here, the rate of pre-symptomatic infected feces). Indeed, if 99% of the data are not pre-symptomatic infected excreta, then a silly algorithm that systematically predicts "this excreta is not pre-symptomatic infected" will have a 99% accuracy! More generally, to estimate the success of a predictive algorithm in a binary prediction task (infected versus not infected), it is necessary to specify two statistics (e.g., base rate and accuracy, or e.g., false positive rate and false negative rate).
Video. How To Update Your Beliefs Systematically - Bayes' Theorem. Veritasium (2017).

[40] This moment is, of course, highly romanticized. In practice, data scientists often have to run and rerun the computations a large number of times, trying to adjust the learning parameters to find a configuration that works well. For example, in this case, Katia might test several neural network architectures, "batch normalization" tricks, different optimizers (SGD, Adam...) with different parameterizations, and so on. The data scientist often ends up progressing little by little, or resigning. But this laborious work is also less spectacular.

[41] In science, and in physics in particular, we sometimes speak of "5 sigmas". This is the signal considered sufficiently significant to be sometimes called a "scientific discovery", although its exact interpretation is in fact complex, even very misleading. In particular, the use of such signals is highly criticized, especially by the so-called *Bayesian* statistics.
Video. P-Value Problems: Crash Course Statistics #22 (2018).
Video. P-values Broke Scientific Statistics—Can We Fix Them? SciShow (2019).

But a 52.4% success rate will do absolutely nothing to help us stop ROVID-19.

Katia then explains that, indeed, the current algorithm is grossly inadequate. However, the 52.4% superiority over 50% is enough to suggest that SmartPoop is indeed picking up a distinctive signal from infected feces.

> If SmartPoop detected absolutely nothing, then you would expect an error rate of 50%, explains Katia. But not exactly 50%, because of statistical fluctuations. Knowing that the test was performed on tens of thousands of excrement videos, we would expect to get 50% plus or minus an error of about 0.5%. However, here we are at 52.4%, or 2.4% more than 50%. So a 2.4% deviation is almost 5 times the 0.5% fluctuation[42]. That's a lot. And it means that the distinction most likely exists! SmartPoop is just not able to clearly identify it *yet*!

Marc asks Katia what is missing to discern this signal. Katia replies:

> If we want to diagnose anything, we need data. A lot of data. And we will also need a lot of machines to analyze all this data. But now that we have five standard deviations, I am sure we will be able to find investors to help us! We have our PoC!

Katia and Marc then decide to throw themselves wholeheartedly into the development of SmartPoop. Katia resigns from her company and spends day and night improving SmartPoop's algorithms, promoting the application and looking for investors. She then rents even more computing power on Amazon Web Service servers, and also calls her former PhD friends to help her develop SmartPoop.

Marc spends his time testing SmartPoop, and suggesting improvements to the interface to make it easier and more understandable for all those users[43]. Marc also regularly contacts different medias, and asks them to promote SmartPoop to gather more users and data. Science4Alpha regularly talks about Smart-Poop's progress in its YouTube videos, and encourages its web colleagues to do the same.

Book. The Equation of Knowledge: From Bayes' Rule to a Unified Philosophy of Science. Lê Nguyên Hoang. CRC Press (2020).

[42]Note that Katia is careful to talk about *fluctuation* interval, not *confidence* interval. These two notions are often mistakenly confused, although they describe quite distinct objects. In the first case, it is an uncertainty on the data to be observed, while in the second case, it is an interval that estimates the values of a parameter of a model, from the observed data. However, this confidence interval should not be confused with a third type of interval, called a *confidence* (or *credibility*) interval. Unlike the confidence interval, the credence interval also takes into account the overall state of scientific knowledge before the data are observed.

[43]In computer science, we talk about UX/UI design, for user experience and user interface.

Day by day, SmartPoop's performance is improving. In July 2020, it goes to 55%. In August, it goes up to 60%. Katia and Marc are now invited on TV shows to talk about SmartPoop. The national newspapers headline: "Film your excrement to get out of lockdown!"

It is then that an investor, called Luke Vaydan, decides to invest 10 million euros for 10% of SmartPoop, of which Katia and Marc then become co-founders. SmartPoop then hired its first developers, in charge of improving the application and SmartPoop's algorithms, as well as sales people to encourage the massive adoption of the application. This money also allows to pay the increasingly important bills of the computing servers.

SmartPoop's triumph

By December 2020, SmartPoop now has nearly 100 million regular users, and several billion videos of excrement reaching a total of 320 years of videos[44]. But most importantly, SmartPoop's performance then reaches 90%. The application is then audited and approved by health authorities, who now encourage its mass adoption. After a full year, in January 2021, the lockdown is finally lifted.

> This is great, says Marc, a guest on Science4Alpha. The basic reproduction number of ROVID-19 is around 8. If we assume that, as soon as an individual is diagnosed positive by SmartPoop, then they and their roommates isolate themselves at home, knowing that the error rate is 10%, then we should divide the reproduction rate by 10, which theoretically brings us back to 0.8. Since 0.8 is below 1, this gives us a chance to contain ROVID-19, without requiring global lockdowns. But of course, these are only estimates. It remains crucial that care is still taken with physical distancing, barrier gestures and diapering. We must also constantly monitor the effective reproduction number that determines how the disease spreads. But, for the first time, there is hope to come back to a normal life.

Gradually, every country in the world is adopting SmartPoop, which is now used by 3 billion people on earth. ROVID-19 is then contained to only a few thousand cases per country. At the end of 2021, the World Health Organization announced it publicly. Thanks to SmartPoop, which is now 99% accurate, ROVID-19 is now declared under control.

---

[44]Every regular user uploads a video a day, for several months, hence the billions of videos. Each video is a few seconds long, which is about 10 billion seconds of video, or about 320 years of video.

To go further

Don't stop there! Check the sequel of the novel or the outline.
If you enjoyed it, please consider sharing and promoting this science fiction
novel to others!

2. Filtering fecal data

The couple leaves the hospital trembling. A few scattered words pronounced by the oncologist[1] a few minutes earlier still echo in their heads. "Therapeutic escape", "bone metastases", "experimental treatments". Lucile Polmon, who accompanied her husband to the consultation, knows these terms by heart. She has already read the definitions on the internet, several times, and she knows too well what it means to the one she loves.

It's okay, he said, holding back tears... It's going to be okay.

Unfortunately, Lucile's husband's false optimism is not enough. Two years later, despite intensive chemotherapy sessions[2], the husband dies, at only 42 years old. He thus abandons Lucile with their only daughter.

Since then, Lucile, deeply traumatized by her husband's cancer, devours all the health information she can find. The day SmartPoop was released, she had immediately downloaded the app. She was one of the first to adopt the app daily. Soon, she forced her 12-year-old daughter, Jeanne, to use SmartPoop as well. Every night now, she reads through her own and her daughter's SmartPoop data, looking for any abnormalities.

Mom, I'm fine. You don't have to keep fixating on this, Jeanne says. You're turning it into an unhealthy obsession. Since we've been using SmartPoop, you're on edge all the time, you hardly eat anymore and I'm sure you don't sleep enough.

The day you get cancer, you won't be laughing so hard.

No one is laughing, Mom. I'm just worried about you.

---

[1] **Video.** What is cancer? What causes cancer and how is it treated. Cancer Treatment Centers of America - CTCA (2013).

[2] **Video.** How does chemotherapy work? - Hyunsoo Joshua No. TED-Ed (2019).

But Lucile's obsession isn't limited to SmartPoop. She spends her days reading
all sorts of health blogs on the web, watching YouTube videos about alternative
medicine and frequenting Facebook groups where strangers share their personal
experiences[3].

Radioactivity in bananas

One night, on her phone, Lucile comes across a YouTube video about the health
impacts of radioactivity, which states that potassium is radioactive. Even
though the video states that this radioactivity is *not* a concern[4], the YouTube
algorithm then recommends[5] another video entitled "Bananas, a GMO designed
to exterminate the population". Curious about such a title, Lucile clicks on the
video. She learns that the modern banana is not natural. According to the
author of the video, bananas are the result of manipulation by food industry
groups[6]. The video also features a masked witness.

> Potassium was injected into natural bananas to remove the seeds
> and make them more appealing for sales, he says. It made billions
> of dollars for the industrial farms. When I proved that potassium
> was radioactive, I received threats. And when I insisted, I was fired.

Two hours later, Lucile is still on her phone[7]. She now discovers Facebook

---

[3]Some scientific studies suggest a strong link between mental distress and beliefs in alternative medicine.
Paper. Are modern health worries associated with medical conspiracy theories? Journal of
Psychosomatic Research. Y Lahrach and A Furnham (2017).
Paper. Belief in a COVID-19 Conspiracy Theory as a Predictor of Mental Health and Well-
Being of Health Care Workers in Ecuador: Cross-Sectional Survey Study. Xi Chen, Stephen X
Zhang, Asghar Afshar Jahanshahi, Aldo Alvarez-Risco, Huiyang Dai, Jizhen Li and Verónica
García Ibarra. JMIR Public Health and Surveillance (2020).

[4]Radioactivity is in fact ubiquitous. What makes it dangerous is not its presence, but the
dose of radioactivity. Of course, the dose in bananas is far too low to be a health concern.
Video. The Most Radioactive Places on Earth. Veritasium (2014).

[5]This recommendation algorithm has become one of the most influential entities in the
world. To see this, it's helpful to note some statistics. Since 2016, there are more views on
YouTube than searches on Google. In 2019 (before COVID-19!), YouTube views represented
one billion viewing hours for two billion humans on earth, or an average of half an hour per
day. Yet YouTube's recommendation algorithm is responsible for 2 out of 3 views. After all,
every time a user goes to YouTube.com or clicks on the YouTube app on their phone, it is this
algorithm that decides which videos will be offered to the user, not to mention the auto-play
or the suggestion bar on the right side of the site. In their book Le Fabuleux Chantier, El
Mahdi El Mhamdi and Lê Nguyên Hoang claim that this makes YouTube's algorithm the
most powerful entity in the world, as it is capable of locking certain populations into their
beliefs, or silencing certain information by never recommending it.
Book. Le fabuleux chantier : Rendre l'intelligence artificielle robustement bénéfique. Lê
Nguyên Hoang et El Mahdi El Mhamdi. EDP Sciences (2019). *English translation pending.*
Web. YouTube (Tournesol Wiki).

[6]**Video.** The Terrifying Truth About Bananas. SciShow (2013).

[7]Web platforms have huge economic interests in making their products addictive so that

groups denouncing the "potassium scandal" and demanding a ban on all products containing potassium, starting with bananas. These sites also explain that consuming magnesium pills reduces potassium levels. "Magnesium destroys potassium particles," some of the messages state.

Three hours later, in the middle of the night, Lucile now discovers a blog that presents magnesium as a miracle cure, not only against radioactive particles, but also against solar storms and their carcinogenic effects[8]. "We have tested and approved it, on thousands of members of our community," the blog states.

It is 4 am when Lucile finally decides to go to bed. Before going to bed, however, she opens the SmartPoop application. There she discovers that SmartPoop provides an estimate of the magnesium and potassium content of feces. "Excellent," she says to herself. "I'm going to be able to monitor my health, and my daughter's health".

She closes her eyes and goes to sleep with a firm resolution. As soon as she wakes up, she will buy magnesium supplements — the blog had a link to a site that sold them[9]. For her health, and even more for her daughter's.

Anything for his daughter

The next evening, before eating, Lucile said to Jeanne: "I want you to take three doses of magnesium a day. One in the morning, one at noon and one in the evening".

Are you sure that's a good idea?

If you don't want to get cancer like Dad did, you need these three doses of magnesium.

users stay on their platforms. This is sometimes referred to as the *attention economy*. In 2021, the *Facebook files*, along with whistleblower Frances Haugen, revealed the fact that, for several years, Facebook has knowingly and systematically prioritized the retention of its users' attention over the risks this endured on their mental health, medical misinformation and geopolitical tensions.

Video. Big Tech's Battle For Our Attention. BrainCraft (2018).

Video. The Social Dilemma. Netflix (2020).

Journal. The Facebook Files. Wall Street Journal (2021).

Video. Facebook Whistleblower Frances Haugen: The 60 Minutes Interview (2021).

[8]Solar storms actually pose serious risks to electrical and electronic systems, and can be very carcinogenic to an astronaut in space, or even to a crew in an airplane. However, at sea level, the Earth's magnetic field largely protects us from its carcinogenic effects.

Video. Could Solar Storms Destroy Civilization? Solar Flares & Coronal Mass Ejections. Kurzgesagt - In a Nutshell (2020).

[9]Many medical misinformation sites are very lucrative, either because they sell alternative medicine directly or because they sell targeted advertising to a vulnerable audience, which they will be able to tarrify at high cost.

Facebook 'still making money from anti-vax sites'. The Guardian (2021).

But the box says not to take more than one dose a day.

Forget what the box says and trust me. You need three doses of magnesium a day. And stay away from bananas too. They are GMOs full of radioactive potassium, produced by capitalist companies.

What? You are completely crazy!

How dare you talk to your mother like that? Apologize!

Calm down and I'll apologize.

Take your three doses and go to bed.

I'll go to bed, but I won't take your three doses. You're completely delirious.

Lucile takes a box of magnesium and throws it at her daughter, who receives it in the eye. Realizing this, Lucile runs to Jeanne to apologize. But Jeanne gets up and runs to her room crying. As she leaves the dining room, she turns to Lucile and says: "You should be ashamed of the way you treat your daughter."

Alone and on the verge of tears, powerless and feeling hated, Lucile finds refuge in the Facebook groups she had frequented the day before[10]. She reads the testimonies of other Internet users who share a similar experience: "My family is blind and naive". "My wife doesn't want to believe me". "I decided to add magnesium directly to the sauce I serve them". This last quote inspires Lucile. To save her daughter and protect her from cancer, Lucile now decides to pour magnesium directly into the food she prepares.

In the days that follow, despite Lucile's repeated apologies, family meals are tense and silent. At the end of each meal, Lucile systematically looks at her daughter's SmartPoop data. To her satisfaction, her magnesium levels are steadily increasing. But Lucile is frustrated to see that potassium levels are not decreasing. After a week, Lucile is still worried. "Potassium is radioactive, and radioactivity causes cancer," she keeps reading on Facebook. Until the

---

[10] According to Christian Picciolini, a former extremist and now active in de-radicalization movements, victims of radicalization are often people who feel sad, helpless, and hateful themselves after suffering what he calls "potholes".
Video. My descent into America's neo-Nazi movement & how I got out | Christian Picciolini | TEDxMileHigh (2017).
Book. Breaking Hate Confronting the New Culture of Extremism. Christian Picciolini. Hachette books (2020).

potassium level is reduced to zero[11], her daughter is at risk of cancer. Lucile finds this unacceptable.

Lucile's Facebook group explains that each individual is unique and that magnesium levels can vary greatly between individuals. In fact, if potassium is not dropping, magnesium doses should be increased. The group adds that the diarrhea that may result is a sign that the treatment is starting to work[12]. Convinced by these explanations, Lucile decides to increase the doses of magnesium, while taking care that the level of magnesium in the excrement never exceeds the threshold considered dangerous by the websites she visits. Week after week, these doses increase. They increase to four doses per day per person, then to six, then to eight. But nothing happens. SmartPoop says Jane has constant diarrhea, but the potassium levels don't go down. Meanwhile, however, magnesium levels do not reach dangerous levels.

One evening, however, after finishing her soup, Jeanne turned pale. She gets up from her chair, takes two steps, then collapses. "Jeanne, Jeanne," Lucile wrote to herself. She calls the emergency services, who take Jeanne to the intensive care unit. Lucile is asked to wait in the waiting room while Jeanne is closely monitored. The doctor finally comes back to Lucile, explaining that Jeanne has unfortunately died of a magnesium overdose.

> This is not possible. I monitor her magnesium levels every day, and they are well below the health-critical levels, Lucile exclaims.

> I don't know what measuring tool you use, but I can assure you that there is nothing normal and healthy about her magnesium level.

The error bars

Katia walks into Marc's office in a huff. "We have a huge problem". She explains to him that SmartPoop has just received a letter from Lucile's lawyer, who explains the story of Jeanne's death.

> The mother is now suing us, adds Katia. She accuses SmartPoop of lying about the amount of magnesium in the feces. By underestimating the risk of overdose, she believes SmartPoop encouraged her to increase the amount of magnesium given to her daughter. According to her, SmartPoop is a co-perpetrator in her daughter's involuntary homicide by negligence[13]. This is nonsense!

---

[11] In fact, a severe potassium deficiency, called hypokalemia, is also dangerous to your health. So is an excess of potassium, called hyperkalemia.

[12] Excess magnesium does lead to diarrhea.
Paper. Fecal Excretion of Soluble Magnesium by Humans. David Saunders and Hugh Wiggins. Western Journal of Medicine (1983).

[13] **Journal.** What Are Homicide and Murder. Expert Law (2018).

And is it true? Did SmartPoop underestimate the magnesium content?

I don't know. I haven't checked the data.

After a silence, Katia adds however:

But yes, it seems likely. We have never trained our algorithms with excreta data with such unusual concentrations of magnesium. The algorithms probably failed to estimate these doses adequately[14].

Can you check the numbers now?

Katia then goes into her office, followed by Marc. She opens her computer, and taps on the keyboard frantically. After a few minutes, she finally finds the information.

I found it. Yes indeed, the dose is underestimated by a factor of ten. However, there is a huge error bar[15] which contains the value found by the doctors. The algorithm is right. We are not wrong.

OK... But Katia, we cannot expect our users to correctly interpret error bars[16]. They don't understand that if you estimate 20 milligrams per liter, with an error bar between 5 and 200, that means

---

[14]Katia highlights here one of the great challenges of algorithm safety, namely the validation of their performance on critical and rare cases (sometimes called *edge cases*). On the one hand, the rarity of these cases means that we have very little data, or sometimes no data at all, to test the security of the algorithm against these cases. On the other hand, the fact that these cases are critical means that the safety of the algorithm for these specific cases can be a matter of life and death. However, even if each rare and critical case is very rare, the set of all rare and critical cases can still be large and occur with a non-negligible probability, especially when the algorithm is used billions of times a day. Unfortunately, as discussed in this paper in the case of autonomous cars, there are not many effective methods for validating an algorithm against rare and critical cases.
Paper. Efficient statistical validation with edge cases to evaluate Highly Automated Vehicles. Dhanoop Karunakaran, Stewart Worrall and Eduardo Nebot. ITSC (2020).

[15]When collecting or analyzing data, it is usually very useful to specify the uncertainty in the data, or in inferred estimates of the data. The easiest way to do this is to report an interval such as "between 5 and 200 milligrams per liter of blood", which ideally corresponds to a credence interval (which is different from a "confidence interval"). Such an interval should then be interpreted as follows: "according to the model used by SmartPoop and knowing the data collected by SmartPoop, SmartPoop estimates that, with 95% credence, the concentration of magnesium in the patient's blood is between 5 and 200 milligrams per liter".

[16]As a real-world example, the accuracy of DNA testing by companies specializing in their sequencing is actually surprisingly poor, to the point where it might be argued to be a dangerous lie. In a report for CBC News, two twin girls received different estimates of their ethnic origins from the same company, after sending in samples of their saliva at the same

it could very well be 5 milligrams per liter or 200 milligrams per liter. Most people are just going to hold on to the 20 milligrams per liter figure[17].

Yeah. Anyways... It's not our fault that some people are dumb[18].

Let's see, Katia...

In any case, we're in trouble. The mother is asking for ten million euros in compensation.

That's a lot! But... we can easily afford it, right?

It is not so simple, Marc. If that happened to one person...

It will happen to many other people too!

We now have 3 billion users. If 0.0001% of them have a story like this, we're going to end up with 3000 lawsuits[19]. We're in big trouble...

---

time! And those estimates were very different from one DNA sequencing company to the next. Intriguingly, one of the companies, 23AndMe, had an option on the credence of the analysis results, which was set at 50% by default (and not particularly highlighted in the user interface). When this credence was moved to 90%, the analysis then provided very vague geographic origins, such as "somewhere in Europe." Regulation seems dangerously lax on what clearly appears to be potentially dangerous misinformation, sold by private companies. **Video.** Twins get 'mystifying' DNA ancestry test results (Marketplace). CBC News (2019).

[17]What Marc is describing here is the difference between reasoning with the extent of ignorance and reasoning with only the (deterministic) model that one thinks is most likely. In Bayesianism, we talk about the difference between the *Bayesian multiverse* (which describes all credible scenarios) and the *maximum a posteriori*. Faced with uncertainty, perhaps because this uncertainty scares us or is too complex, we often tend to reason with the latter rather than the former. **Book.** How to Decide: Simple Tools for Making Better Choices. Annie Duke. Portfolio (2020).

[18]Blaming users (and their mistakes) is a recurring excuse for web companies to avoid taking responsibility for poor user experience design. Typically, they might argue that it is not their *fault* if users "prefer" conspiracy content. However, the search for a single fault is here arguably misleading and inappropriate. Rather, it seems more appropriate to ponder who could do what, or who could be reasonably forced to do what, in order to avoid dangerous harm for many. In fact, most laws actually largely frame this. If a dealer sells a product to a customer knowing full well that the use of that product by that customer will endanger the customer or others, then they usually have a legal responsibility in that endangerment of others (see footnote[^homicide]).

[19]This is what Lê Nguyên Hoang calls the "N epsilon" effect. If a very small risk (of probability epsilon) affects a very large number of individuals, then our intuition will generally be very inadequate to determine whether the population-wide risk is large or negligible, because our intuition often has a very poor intuition of very large numbers and very small numbers. It is then appropriate to try to pause the calculation, to better estimate the risks. **Video.** Millions of billions of dilemmas. Science4All (2021).

SmartPoop's responsibility

After a long silence, Marc then asks, "Katia, do you think we're responsible for this death? Are we really guilty of manslaughter?"

We saved millions, maybe even billions of lives, by diagnosing ROVID-19. SmartPoop is a cool product. It's completely unfair to think that SmartPoop had anything to do with a homicide[20]!

Yes, but can killing a young girl be justified by saving a million others[21]?

Marc, we didn't kill that girl. Stop messing around. Our algorithm didn't even make a mistake! It's mostly her mother who is crazy enough to fill her with magnesium! It's not our fault if she can't interpret error bars correctly.

Certainly. But from a certain point of view we helped her to do it. It's a bit as if someone wanted to commit suicide, and was handed them a gun to do it[22].

Easy Marc. And above all, don't you dare saying that in court.

Doesn't it bother you, Katia, that this young girl died, and that SmartPoop seems to have a share of responsibility in this death?

What do you mean, "a share of the responsibility"? We didn't do anything wrong! And then, there are many other causes in this case,

---

[20]This remark appeals to the notion of moral credit, the idea that having acted very morally in the past justifies less moral actions in the future.
Video. Moral Licensing. Mind Field S3E2. VSauce (2018).

[21]Marc poses here a classical (and in fact way too caricatured) question of moral philosophy, opposing deontology to utilitarianism.
Video. Would you sacrifice one person to save five? - Eleanor Nelsen. TED-Ed (2017).
Video. The Trolley Problem in Real Life. Mind Field. VSauce (2017).

[22]It is interesting to note that the carrying and even selling of weapons is prohibited for the general public in most democracies around the world, probably because these technologies represent a danger to others, and even to oneself if misused. One could make the observation that, in a similar way, many information technologies today are misused and represent a danger to others, especially when they promote massive hate speech, cyber-harassment or medical misinformation which, in times of COVID-19, can lead to sustained pandemics and to dangerous and constraining sanitary restrictions for all.

such as the conspiracy theories that this mother swallowed. Comparatively, we have nothing to do with it[23]. We only give perfectly objective statistics[24].

I mean, "contrafactually[25]". In a world where this mother didn't have access to SmartPoop, she probably wouldn't have dared to give her daughter so much magnesium. Without SmartPoop, this young girl would probably still be alive.

First, you can't know at all[26]. I'm sure that even without SmartPoop, people would be messing around with supplements. And in this game, Facebook and YouTube seem to me to be much more responsible than us[27]. The misinformation shared on these platforms is what caused this whole thing in the first place[28].

---

[23]Katia underlines here the *multifactorial* aspect of Jeanne's death. More generally, the idea of identifying *one* cause or *one* culprit (or at least *one* responsible) seems limited to monofactorial contexts. However, the complexity of modern information flows and the fact that it integrates many entities makes monocausal reasoning flawed for analyzing what should be done in the future to avoid such tragic situations. A more systemic approach seems necessary.

[24]Algorithms are sometimes considered "objective". If you think about it, what makes them more "reliable" is rather their transparency (if they are open source), or at least the reproducibility of their calculations. However, it may be misleading to see them as purely objective, since an alternative algorithm could have been used (especially in the context of machine learning), and it might have led to very different conclusions. At least it can be said that the statistics computed and reported by the algorithm are subject to the choice of the algorithm used to make which statistical estimates and to decide how to display the results (and indeed, a large part of information ethics is determining which algorithms are preferable to deploy on a large scale). In any case, even if a statistic is objective, it is not necessarily *desirable* to communicate, especially since statistics can be extremely misleading, and end up guiding many decisions.
Video. This is How Easy It Is to Lie With Statistics. Zach Star (2019).
Book. Weapons of Math Destruction: How Big Data Increases Inequality and Threatens Democracy. Cathy O'Neil. Penguin (2017).

[25]When judging a decision X, contrafactual reasoning involves comparing the likely consequences of doing X, to the likely consequences of not doing X (or doing an alternative to X). This is the approach often favored by decision theory, especially in the presence of uncertainty.
Book. How to Decide: Simple Tools for Making Better Choices. Annie Duke. Portfolio (2020).

[26]Note that in Bayesianism, an increasingly popular epistemology, a rational agent cannot know "can't know at all". Instead, they will have a so-called *prior belief* on what future or counterfactual scenarios are more probable, based on their past experience and their scientific knowledge. In particular, this will lead them to provide a probabilistic guess on the advent of any future or counterfactual event.
Book. The Equation of Knowledge: From Bayes' Rule to a Unified Philosophy of Science. Lê Nguyên Hoang. CRC Press (2020).

[27]The regulation of information distribution platforms, especially with regard to false information, remains a delicate legal blur.
Journal. Is Facebook a publisher? In public it says no, but in court it says yes. The Guaridan (2018).

[28]The central role of these platforms, and in particular their algorithms, in the current mis-

Katia, I think you are much too focused on the business and on protecting SmartPoop. At the end of the day, SmartPoop's goal is not to make money or protect our image, it's to save lives, and to avoid causing harm[29].

Marc, you are thinking too much in the short term. If you want SmartPoop to save lives, SmartPoop must live on. The day Smart-Poop is dismantled or goes bankrupt, if there's another ROVID-19 pandemic, it won't be about the life of some nutcase's daughter; it will be a matter of millions, if not billions, of lives[30].

Visibly both frustrated, Katia and Marc mark a silence in their discussion.

In the meantime, I still think that Facebook and YouTube should be prosecuted more than we are, Katia adds.

Marc remains silent. After a minute, he speaks again.

That might be a possible defense. We can accept some damages, but on the condition that the lawsuits are also brought against Facebook and YouTube, or any other social media used by the mother[31].

---

information crisis is the central topic of a previous book by Lê Nguyên Hoang, co-authored with researcher El Mahdi El Mhamdi, and of articles published in sociology and philosophy.
Book. Le fabuleux chantier : Rendre l'intelligence artificielle robustement bénéfique. Lê Nguyên Hoang et El Mahdi El Mhamdi. EDP Sciences (2019). *English translation pending.*
Paper. Science Communication Desperately Needs More Aligned Recommendation Algorithms. Lê Nguyên Hoang. Frontiers in Communication (2020).
Paper. Recommendation Algorithms, a Neglected Opportunity for Public Health. Lê Nguyên Hoang, Louis Faucon & El-Mahdi El-Mhamdi. Revue Médecine et Philosophie (2021).

[29] This remark echoes the *facebook files*, which reveal that, on numerous occasions, Facebook management prioritized profits and corporate image over the tragedies its platform was compounding.
Journal. The facebook files. Wall Street Journal (2021).

[30] While some call for the dismantling of large digital companies, others point to the fact that such dismantling runs the risk of leading to even more worrisome unintended side effects, such as the inability to moderate the flow of information, including dangerous and compromising information, such as pedo-pornographic images, calls for racial hatred, or cyber-bullying. This is the case, for example, of Sinan Aral, a professor at MIT, who has studied disinformation on social medias extensively.
Book. The Hype Machine: How Social Media Disrupts Our Elections, Our Economy, And Our Health-and How We Must Adapt. Sinan Aral. Penguin (2021).

[31] What Katia is suggesting here could be a solution to better align the interests of corporate employees to promote ethics. Instead of asking them to highlight the ethical dilemmas of their own companies (which nevertheless seems important and desirable, but is in practice affected by *ethics washing*), these employees could be paid to highlight the ethical problems with their competitors' products. In practice, a huge barrier to this is access to competitors' data, without which the identification of ethical problems is often impossible.

SmartPoop's commitment

Katia and Marc then organize a meeting with their lawyers to prepare an action plan along these lines. They added that, in response to the lawsuit, and to avoid other future lawsuits, SmartPoop was committed to being a major player in the fight against misinformation.

> The goal is that future complaints will be directed more towards Facebook and YouTube than towards us, explains Katia.

> It's not going to be easy, warns the lawyer. The mother doesn't seem to consider the information she read to be false information. I'm not sure she's going to be willing to file a lawsuit against them. But we can try to find other victims of misinformation and file a class action suit. This may convince Lucile to sue these other companies too.

Months later, the trial takes place. The verdict comes in. SmartPoop is found to be a co-perpetrator in the involuntary homicide of Jeanne. However, the co-perpetrators are many, as they include numerous social medias that spread huge amounts of dangerous medical misinformation. A compensation of one million euros is demanded from SmartPoop. In addition, the court asks SmartPoop to take responsibility for the misinformation published in the application, but also for the risks of misunderstanding by a public that is not trained to understand medical data.

In response to the court's request, Katia and Mark agreed to hire Lucile as a consultant, and to work with doctors, psychologists and graphic designers to improve the design of the SmartPoop application and to offer simple, secure and easily understandable health check-ups[32]. After weeks of sometimes tense discussions and hard work, a new design for SmartPoop was established. Science4Alpha invites Marc to present the new SmartPoop design on his YouTube channel.

> SmartPoop is turning into an anomaly alert app, with safe medical recommendations, Marc explains. Rather than drowning the user in a sea of data in which they could get lost, the app will now

---

[32]We can emphasize what this sentence implies. In practice, whether information is misinformation or not is a very complex issue, requiring an understanding of the psychology of the audience, and in particular their likely misinterpretations. A company that wants to achieve this must hire highly skilled teams capable of responding to this delicate task, which will inevitably be very costly. Having said this, technology companies often already invest a lot to optimize the user experience, even the addiction of users to their products.
Video. How a handful of tech companies control billions of minds every day | Tristan Harris. TED (2017).
Video. The Social Dilemma. Netflix (2020).

accompany users. In the case of very well identified risks, such as constipation and diarrhea, or for certain deficiencies such as vitamin A deficiencies that we are now able to detect very well, SmartPoop will notify the user[33] and provide a medical recommendation, in accordance with what has been decided with the *Centers for Disease Control and Prevention*. Typically, this will be a recommendation of the form "please drink more water" or "remember to eat carrots", and sometimes "please check a doctor".

What happens if an anomaly is found, but there is no simple agreed-upon recommendation to cure it?

Excellent question! In this case, SmartPoop will simply recommend consulting a doctor[34]. What we want above all is to do no harm. *Primum non nocere*, as they say in medicine. In other words, the priority is to do no harm. SmartPoop now implements this principle with great rigor.

Is the raw data from SmartPoop still available?

Yes, in accordance with the General Data Protection Regulation (GDPR), all data collected by SmartPoop remains accessible to the user. But we have decided to be very careful about the way they are presented, so that users are more wary, especially of the inevitable measurement errors of our device. Our learning algorithms are still improving their estimates of the physicochemical properties of feces from photographs, and we are well aware that on many tasks the reliability of these algorithms is not yet there. That is why we are very careful that such data are presented with many error bars. We prefer that users become aware of the uncertainty of our models before they read the results of the analysis of these models[35].

---

[33] In 2013, the U.S. *Food and Drug Admnistration* (FDA) banned the DNA sequencing company 23AndMe from sharing the results of their genetic tests with their patients, due to a lack of convincing studies on the reliability of the tests.
Journal. FDA bans 23andme personal genetic tests. BBC (2013).

[34] On their website, the company 23AndMe now puts a lot of emphasis on the need to consult a doctor with their test results, and even before deciding to sequence one's DNA. In October 2021, they wrote, "**These reports are not a substitute for visiting a medical professional**. Consult a health care professional to help you interpret and use the genetic results. The results should **not** be used to make medical decisions." And added, "We encourage you to speak with a genetic counselor."
Web. 23andMe Genetic Health Risk Reports: What you should know.

[35] More generally, research in AI safety places great emphasis on allowing algorithms to measure their own uncertainty about the results they compute.
Paper. Benchmarking Uncertainty Estimation Methods for Deep Learning With Safety-Related Metrics. Maximilian Henne, Adrian Schwaiger, Karsten Roscher, Gereon Weiss.

Marc, you also say that you take measures against misinformation?

Yes, absolutely. We have also worked closely with doctors, psychologists, graphic designers, but also with patients, to provide Smart-Poop with quality medical information, either directly in the application or via links to trusted websites. Lucile's case has shown us that this is a major public health issue.

But what is misinformation? Is it misinformation to say that bananas are not natural and that they are radioactive?

What we discovered with Lucile's story is that the notion of misinformation is in fact annoyingly subtle[36]. On the one hand, it's not quite a fake news as some would say. But on the other hand, said in the wrong context, this sentence can be misleading for some audiences, if they are then led to believe that bananas are therefore dangerous, or that it is better to stay away from them[37]. To be clear, yes, bananas have been modified by agriculture. For 7000 years we have been selecting the banana varieties that suit us, it is not natural at all. But this is the case with almost all the food we eat, from wheat to beef, apples, oranges and yes, bananas too. And yes, bananas are radioactive too. But the radioactivity of a banana is two hundred times less than what you get if you take a plane for a 6 hour trip, just because the plane is flying a little high in the sky. If you are afraid of the radioactivity of the banana, you should be terrified of the plane. By the way, there is a unit, the BED, for "banana equivalent dose", which is used in a didactic way to present some very low exposure to radioactivity[38].

Unfortunately, as an educational YouTuber, I can assure you that explaining all this takes time[39]...

SafeAI@AAAI (2020).

Book. Human Compatible: Artificial Intelligence and the Problem of Control. Stuart Russell. Penguin (2019).

This point also seems paramount for humans, including experts who often err on the side of overconfidence.

Video. Soldiers and Scouts: Why our minds weren't built for truth I Julia Galef. Long Now Foundation (2019).

Video. Why you don't need certainty to be influential. Julia Galef (2021).

[36]**Book.** The Reality Game How the Next Wave of Technology Will Break the Truth. Samuel Woolley. PublicAffairs (2020).

[37]**Paper.** Teaching beyond verifying sources and "fake news": Critical media education to challenge media injustices. Jeremy Stoddard, Jonathan Tunstall, Leila Walker & Emily Wight. Journal of Media Literacy Education (2021).

[38]**Video.** The Most Radioactive Places on Earth. Veritasium (2014).

[39]"Brandolini's law", also known as the principle of asymmetry of idiocy, asserts that the

Yes, and the public's attention is very limited. That's why, rather than inundating SmartPoop users with complex information, we've opted to give them only very simple and reliable information, while adding links to more complete information.

Now for the big announcement in this video. Marc, you are now my boss.

Yes indeed. Science4Alpha, you are an exceptional educator, who supported us very early in our approach, and who is yourself very concerned by public health issues. We have decided to officially support your work by guaranteeing you a stable income. And we've made similar agreements with nine other science YouTubers. We are very excited about these partnerships because we believe that quality information is a priority for public health[40].

But, Marc, as some are probably writing in the comments, aren't there risks of conflicts of interest?

Always. We have done our best to find a system that allows you to keep a close eye on us and live comfortably, while guaranteeing you the freedom that scientific communication work requires, especially on sensitive subjects such as public health. In particular, we have committed to guaranteeing one year's income in case of breach of contract with you or your colleagues[41], and we have no right of

---

cost of deconstructing an erroneous belief is orders of magnitude greater than the cosf of spreading the erroneous belief. This makes the rectification of erroneous beliefs extremely difficult, especially when confronted with the piling of shaky arguments in defense of a belief.

[40]The appropriateness of such collaborations, with private or government institutions, is an ongoing dilemma for science communication, especially knowing how little funding it receives at the moment, and how difficult it is to access information internal to large companies. One example is this collaboration between science YouTuber SmarterEveryDay and 23AndMe, which is a collaboration framework that the science YouTuber found satisfactory.
Video. DNA Testing and Privacy (Behind the scenes at the 23andMe Lab) - Smarter Every Day (2017).
Especially on controversial topics, such collaborations can have counterproductive effects on trust in science communicators.
Paper. Trust in scientists in times of pandemic: Panel evidence from 12 countries. Yann Algan, Daniel Cohen, Eva Davoine, Martial Foucault & Stefanie Stantcheva. PNAS (2021).
For example, Lê Nguyên Hoang, one of the authors of this book, produced a video in collaboration with the French Ministry of Health, which received more dislikes than likes, thus questioning the relevance of such a collaboration.
Video. Un vaccin pour permettre aux étudiants de retrouver leur vie d'avant (ft. Prof. Fischer). Science4All (2021).

[41]Employees of Google's AI ethics team did not have that luxury. In particular, Timnit Gebru was fired on vacation, without notice, shortly after she wrote an academic research paper critical of the language algorithms in which Google had invested heavily. Science4All (2020).

control over the content you publish[42].

Do you hear that, dear viewers? I promise, I will remain free in what I say. If SmartPoop screws up its product or its new interface, and nevertheless deploys it at scale, I'll be the first to report it.

I hope so, yes. Our relationship with you is going to be very much based on trust. We trust you, and your willingness to prioritize public health in your videos, over, say, clickbaitness. And we hope that you, Science4Alpha, as well as the general public and our various partners, will trust our commitment to public health above all[43].

Shall we take a little selfie with a check to finish this video? And yes, we avoid shaking hands, because we still don't have the guarantee that the ROVID-19 is completely gone. So, thanks Marc, and to you viewers, I hope you're as excited as I am to get a view inside SmartPoop. Of course, I won't be able to tell you everything, because some subjects are sensitive, and there are even stories of insider trading that I prefer to avoid[44]. But I promise, we won't be soft on Marc and Katia, especially if they slip up.

We'll try not to slip up too much then!

To make sure you don't miss future videos on public health and algorithmic challenges, don't forget to subscribe, set the bell and feel free to share this video. And I'll see you soon, on Science4Alpha.

To go further

Don't stop there! Check the sequel of the novel or the outline.
If you enjoyed it, please consider sharing and promoting this science fiction novel to others!

---

[42]Note that this is not the case for Google's AI ethics researchers, whose publications are subject to internal approval by senior Google managers. As we saw with the dismissals of Timnit Gebru and Margarett Mitchell, this lack of independence between ethics and Google management is a serious risk to the integrity of Google's research.
Video. Google is dismantling its ethics (and nobody cares...). Science4All (2021).

[43]One of the great difficulties of such a partnership, especially for companies or governments, is trust in the scientific communicator. The communicator could be paid by competitors to produce harmful misinformation. Unfortunately, setting up such partnerships is complicated...

[44]Transparency is a complicated subject too...

3. The turd bias

True comfort is not just knowing that you can relieve yourself safely;
it is knowing that your health will be taken care of at all times thanks
to the intelligence of your toilet. SmartToilets[1] from SmartPoop.
Let us take care of you.

This is the fifth time today that Issa Gueye has seen this ad on his phone. Iron-
ically, this time, he is sitting on the toilet[2], between two videos of comedians,
that he is exposed to it. A few minutes later, when he opens the SmartPoop
application to film his excrement, he realizes that installing SmartToilets would
save him the trouble of filming the turds himself. Even though he's been doing it almost daily for three years now, he still finds the effort laborious and
repulsive.

Issa, the avid sportsman who likes to track his fitness, then clicks on the special
offer offered by his app. As a regular user since the beginning of SmartPoop, he
indeed has a 30% discount on the purchase of a basic SmartToilet, for a total
price of 12,000 euros. It's expensive, but this finance trader can afford it. In
fact, Issa then discovered the existence of a SmartToilet Deluxe version. This
version allows pre-heating of the bowl, odor filtration by ceramic honeycomb
filter, cleaning by fine water jet and drying by hot air, all optimized by artificial
intelligence algorithms to maximize the user's well-being[3]. Intrigued, Issa opts
for this product, despite its exorbitant price of 25,000 euros.

---

[1] SmartToilets are already in development! They even led to an academic publication, with
a prototype capable of. . . rectal recognition!
Paper. A mountable toilet system for personalized health monitoring via the analysis of
excreta. Seung-min Park et al. Nature Biomedical Engineering (2020).

[2] The invention of toilets, and in particular sewage systems, was in fact one of the great
advances in the history of civilization, as it effectively fought the spread of many diseases such
as cholera. In fact, more than 2 billion people still do not have access to it. It is estimated
that, because of this, about 800,000 children die every year from diarrhea.
Video. How The Toilet Changed History. It's Okay to Be Smart (2017).

[3] In Japan, toilets often have several of these features.
Video. Why You Need to Try a High-Tech Japanese Toilet. Lifehacker (2019).

Poo

A few days later, SmartPoop's SmartToilet Deluxe is delivered and installed at Issa's home. That evening, Issa went to test his new toilet with a big smile and some hesitation. As he approaches the toilet, the lid opens automatically. Issa then sits down on the bowl. A strange feeling of warmth accompanies his contact with the bowl. "It's like I'm using the toilet right after someone else. . . Not very reassuring. But I should probably just get used to it," he says to himself.

Hello Issa, says a male voice.

Issa is startled. The toilet has just spoken to him!

Relax and enjoy the comfort of the SmartToilet Deluxe, she explains. I'm Poo, your voice assistant. Would you prefer I use a female voice[4]?

Issa is very disturbed. After a few seconds, he answers: "Yes, I prefer a female voice".

Feel free to tell me how you feel so I can optimize your comfort, says Poo, now with a female voice[5].

Disturbed, Issa remains silent for a few more seconds. He finally replies: "Perhaps we can start by being on a first-name basis.

With pleasure, Issa. I am at your service.

Issa's phone suddenly vibrates. He picks it up. It reads: "Congratulations! You are now using our SmartToilet Deluxe. We wish you a pleasant experience". Still tense, Issa finds it hard to let go.

---

[4] After many criticisms about reinforcing gender bias, Apple decided to give Siri a male voice by default.
Journal. How AI bots and voice assistants reinforce gender bias. Caitlin Chin and Mishaela Robison. Brookings (2020).
Journal. Apple's Siri is no longer a woman by default, but is this really a win for feminism?. Eleonore Fournier-Tombs. The Conversation (2021).

[5] This example highlights the tension between users' control over the technologies they use and the consequences that this control can have on a social scale. Thus, by allowing the user to customize their technologies, there is a risk that they aggravate, consciously or not, gender bias (in this case), hate speech or misinformation. In the end, this tension resides in John Stuart Mill's harm principle; or more simply put, in the principle "the freedoms of some end where those of others begin".
Video. The Harm Principle: How to live your life the way you want to. BBC Radio 4 (2014).

The first time is never easy. But relax. Try to enjoy your new daily comfort.

I'm not used to talking to a voice assistant in the toilet!

I understand. I'm not yet used to talking to toilet users either!

Little by little, however, Issa is increasingly perceiving his SmartToilets as an important new comfort[6]. After all, put together, humans spend an enormous amount of time sitting on a toilet. Might as well make a good time of it!

Finally, Issa moves on with his task.

Uh... Issa says, with some hesitation. Are you... analyzing it?

Yes Issa, I am filming your "data" from different angles, and putting the videos on your online account. I am also taking other samples for further analysis. Do you want to know more?

Yes, tell me more.

With pleasure. The water in which the excreta is bathed is also constantly sampled and analyzed by spectroscopy. In other words, we study the way this water absorbs different colors of the light spectrum, in a very precise way. This allows us to identify certain molecules within your feces, which enables us to do a much more accurate health check-up[7]. We also perform mass spectrometry[8], and chemical measurements, for example of the acidity of this water[9].

When will I have results?

I'll keep you posted, in the bathroom or in your app, if there are any measurements of concern.

---

[6]Billions of humans on earth don't have access to this comfort. As we have seen, this poses serious health problems.
Video. 6 Toilets From History, and What They Taught Us. SciShow (2021). But research is developing solutions to make this comfort available to more people, including innovations in excreta treatment.
Video. 3 Groundbreaking New Toilets. SciShow (2018).

[7]**Video.** Spectrophotometry and Beer's Law. Professor Dave Explains (2019).

[8]Mass spectrometry involves slicing a molecule to be analyzed into charged sub-molecules, for example using electron ionization, and measuring the ability of a magnetic field to deflect the path of sub-molecules. Since heavier submolecules are harder to deflect, this gives us information on the mass of these submolecules, and thus on the mass and composition of the molecule to be analyzed.
Video. IR Spectroscopy and Mass Spectrometry: Crash Course Organic Chemistry #5 (2020).

[9]The acidity of a liquid is measured by its pH, typically via electrical measurements. How a pH meter works! pH Professor (2017).

"Very concerning."

A few days later, when he has just returned home after a hard day's work. Issa receives a notification from SmartPoop. Issa then asks, "Poo, what's going on?"

> I've been running some very concerning tests. Issa, I think you should go to the hospital.

Terrified, Issa leaves his house, gets into his car and drives straight to the hospital. When he arrives at the emergency room, he asks to see a doctor. "For what reason?" he id asked. "I got an alert from SmartPoop, which just told me to come to the emergency room," Issa explains.

After a minute or two, Issa is taken care of.

> Hello Mister Gueye, I'm Dr. Paola Marta. You should know that we are used to dealing with SmartPoop emergencies. For the past two years, most of our patients have come in as a result of a SmartPoop alert, and the report they send us always helps us a lot in caring for our patients[10]. How do you feel?

> So far, all I have is a stomach ache. But I'm pretty terrified. Smart-Poop says my condition is "very concerning."

> Very concerning, you say?

> Yes. Doctor, do you know what's wrong with me and if I'll be okay?

Dr. Marta looks away from Issa. Clearly embarrassed, Dr. Marta seems terrified by SmartPoop's diagnosis. She has had 27 patients whose condition were

---

[10] According to a recent study, most people do indeed seem to trust an algorithm's judgments more than a human's, at least for some predictions like Tesla's success, European sanctions against cyberwarfare, or the future of Brexit. Disturbingly, however, experienced professionals, on the other hand, trust algorithms less, leading them to worse judgments than non-professionals when given an algorithmic advice!

Paper. Algorithm appreciation: People prefer algorithmic to human judgment. Jennifer Logg, Julia Minsona & Don Moore. Organizational Behavior and Human Decision Processes (2019).

Having said this, psychological research also suggests that what is familiar to us seems more believable, and sometimes disturbingly so. This is known as *familiarity bias*. For example, a subject who is repeatedly exposed to the phrase "the body temperature of a chicken" has a greater probability of judging the phrase "the body temperature of a chicken is 34°C" to be true. The fact that Dr. Paola Marta interacts daily with SmartPoop reports, which are also effective in guiding her in the treatment of her patients, could then explain why Dr. Paola Marta trusts SmartPoop.

Video. The Illusion of Truth. Veritasium (2016).

deemed "of great concern" by SmartPoop. All died[11]. After an interminable silence, Dr. Marta finally answered, obviously with an effort to sound as reassuring as possible, despite the circumstances.

I promise you that we will do our best.

After a blood test, Issa finally finds himself lying in a hospital bed, alone, abandoned to his own imagination. He fears the worst. He thinks of all the things he would have liked to have done. Issa harbors regrets, and contemplates his posterity. All his life, Issa has only followed the lure of gain. He was told that to succeed in finance is to roll in gold and triumph in life. This is what he did. Does it make him a bad person[12]?

Certainly, his career has at least allowed him to afford all sorts of luxury gear, like SmartToilets Deluxes. The ultimate proof of social success. But has Issa really accomplished anything in his life? What about all those other people who have suffered because of him? What about his ex-wife, whom he abandoned? Of his children with whom he spent so little time[13]?

Dr. Marta then turns back to Issa. "Finally," Issa exclaims inwardly, feeling as if he has been abandoned for several hours, even though Dr. Marta has only been gone for ten minutes[14]. Dr. Marta then asks Issa to accompany her for an X-ray, and tells him that a colonoscopy is also being considered. In the space of a few hours, Issa will in fact undergo all sorts of analyses. At the end of the day, Dr. Marta tells him that he will stay overnight for observation. She

---

[11]Laplace's law of succession suggests that, if one had a priori total initial uncertainty that a "very concerning" SmartPoop diagnosis led to a life-threatening condition, then, knowing that the first 27 patients with that diagnosis all died, the probability that Issa would in turn die would then be 28/29. This fully justifies Dr. Marta's fear.

Video. Binomial distributions | Probabilities of probabilities, part 1. 3Blue1Brown (2020).

[12]Empirical psychology suggests that self-labeling can give an impression of permanence of some of our properties, which can then be very detrimental to our personal development. This is called a "fixed mindset". In contrast, people who think they can grow (*growth mindset*) seem to be much more fulfilled. Therefore, rather than calling oneself a "bad person", it would seem more appropriate to call oneself a "person who has done some bad things", or even a "person who aspires to do better things".

Video. The power of believing that you can improve | Carol Dweck. TED (2014).

Book. Mindset: The New Psychology of Success. Carol Dweck. Penguin (2007).

[13]These questions refer to what some people call *goal factoring* or *self alignment*, which involves asking ourselves whether the goals we have set are really the goals we would really like to set for ourselves.

Blog. Goal Factoring. LessWrong (2018).

Indeed, it often seems to be the case that these goals are *orphan beliefs*, i.e. goals that we set as a result of fundamental motivations, and that we persist in setting even though these fundamental motivations have disappeared. Typically, we may have wanted to please our parents, at a time when our parents' pride was very important to us; but upon reflection, we came to realize that other fundamental motivations prevailed over that, like, say, actually making the world a better place.

Video. Your brain is not a Bayes net (and why that matters). Julia Galef (2016).

[14]**Video.** How Your Brain Makes Time Pass Fast or Slow. It's Okay To Be Smart (2020).

encourages him to try to eat the meal that is served to him, and to try to get some sleep to rest.

The next morning, Dr. Marta finally arrives in Issa's room. Issa is exhausted. Terrified, he has not slept all night.

What is the news, doctor?

You clearly have very advanced fatigue and a high level of stress, with obvious digestive and sleep problems. Something is wrong. However, all our measurements still fail to identify the origin of your problems. We have called SmartPoop, whose health report is not really in line with our review. They are in the process of manually analyzing your data. We're hoping that together we'll be able to pinpoint the problem. But this is going to take us some time. I'm sorry about that. I'm so sorry.

SmartPoop Alert

At the end of the morning, it's Marc's turn to enter Katia's office.

We have a problem, he says.

What's going on, Marc?

My assistant just told me that a doctor, Dr. Marta, kept trying to reach us last night and this morning. She has a patient whom SmartPoop told to go to the emergency room. They've run a lot of tests on the patient. But they can't figure out what's causing the problem.

Did you get the diagnostics team on the problem?

Yes. They've been working since 9:00 this morning, and they still can't find the problem. They asked me to ask you to take a look at the data.

Are you sure it's my job to look? I'm very busy. I have to prepare for SmartPoopCon 2024 this weekend.

They have an idea of the problem, but they want your expertise to confirm their intuition...

Can you send me the case references?

It's already done.

Katia then opens her email client, which tells her that she has 25,251 unread messages. She sorts her messages by recipient and finds the one from Marc[15]. Katia copies and pastes the case references, and runs queries to the SmartPoop database. She then retrieves Issa's data, and analyzes the statistics of his excrements. Katia executes some commands, which then generate all kinds of graphs. After seeing about fifteen graphs, Katia exclaims: "Oh no! Issa is out of distribution[16]".

What do you mean?

Issa Gueye's video data are perfectly normal. It is his spectrographic data that is reported as "very concerning". But I'm afraid that's because Issa Gueye is a statistically very different SmartToilet Deluxe user from other SmartToilet Deluxe users.

He's Senegalese.

Oh no... I think we have a big problem. Do you have the doctor's number? We need to call her right away.

---

[15]The philosopher Michel Serres liked to insist on the impact of information technologies, such as paper, printing or computers, on the *externalization* of our cognition. In this regard, it is remarkable to note to what extent our email boxes have managed to externalize a large part of our memory. In a sense, our email boxes know us much better than we know ourselves, not because they are "intelligent", but simply because their memory is much more reliable than human memory, and because searching in these email boxes is often much more efficient than searching in our memory.
Video. Michel Serres - Les nouvelles technologies : révolution culturelle et cognitive. I Moved to Diaspora (2012).

[16]So-called "out-of-distribution" data are data that are very distinct from all other data. They are often considered erroneous or even adversarial, so many learning algorithms seek to eliminate them.
Paper. Machine Learning with Adversaries: Byzantine Tolerant Gradient Descent. Peva Blanchard, El Mahdi El Mhamdi, Rachid Guerraoui & Julien Stainer. NIPS (2017).
Paper. A Simple Unified Framework for Detecting Out-of-Distribution Samples and Adversarial Attacks. Kimin Lee, Kibok Lee, Honglak Lee & Jinwoo Shin. NeurIPS (2018).
Security-driven algorithms are usually designed to ignore out-of-distribution data, which therefore leads them to ignore minorities. In fact, as discussed in the following article, there is a fundamental tension between inclusion and security. To resolve this tension, it is critical to better understand distributions (and model our well-founded priors), to better secure and authenticate data sources, or to be much more modest in our algorithm design.
Paper. Collaborative learning in the jungle. El-Mahdi El-Mhamdi, Sadegh Farhadkhani, Rachid Guerraoui, Arsany Guirguis, Lê Nguyên Hoang & Sébastien Rouault. NeurIPS (2021).

Nocebo effect

Marc dials Dr. Marta's number.

Hello Dr. Marta, this is Marc Rofstein. You are currently on speakerphone with Katia Crapinski and myself, President and Vice President of SmartPoop. We have an update on Issa Gueye's case.

Hello Dr. Marta, this is Katia. I've analyzed Mr. Gueye's case, and I'm pretty sure it's a false positive. In other words, SmartPoop made a mistake in reporting a problem with Mr Gueye's data.

Hello Marc and Katia, replies Dr. Marta. Are you sure of what you are saying? Mr. Gueye has some worrying symptoms, especially on the digestive level and in terms of fatigue.

This is weird. The data I have doesn't seem to suggest symptoms of concern, says Katia.

It may be a *nocebo* effect, says Marc.

A *nocebo* effect? Yes, this could be it, indeed, exclaims Dr. Marta.

A *nocebo* effect, asks Katia, what's that?

When a patient thinks that something horrible is going to happen to him, they often develop the symptoms they fear, explains Marc. Digestive symptoms, for example, are quite likely. Mr. Gueye probably trusts SmartPoop so much that when SmartPoop told him it was very concerned about his condition, his condition became very concerning[17].

But explain to me, asks Dr. Marta. Why was his case of false positive? Until now, whenever SmartPoop declared a case of "highly concerning" in our hospital, it always ended up in the intensive care unit, and then in death. That's why I panicked about Mr. Gueye myself - which probably contributed to his *nocebo*.

We just rolled out the SmartToilets and SmartToilets Deluxe, says Katia. I think that the SmartToilets make quite reliable diagnostics. But the Deluxe version has even more advanced sensors, which have not been used as much as the basic SmartToilets. And that's why it's not quite as reliable.

---

[17]**Video.** This Video Will Hurt. CGP Grey (2013).

I understand, thank you, says Dr. Marta. I'll let Mr. Gueye know. Hopefully, it will help cure his *nocebo*. Can I ask you to manually correct his SmartPoop?

It's... done, says Katia, after entering some commands on her computer.

Thank you very much! Have a nice day, concludes Dr. Marta, before hanging up.

163 false positives

Katia hangs up twice, to verify that Dr. Marta is no longer connected. Katia then types several new commands, which display three new graphs. She turns to Marc.

Well done Katia. Always there to rescue us, exclaims Marc.

Marc, I don't think you realize yet how crappy of a situation we are in.

I'm getting fed up with such phrasings. Isn't the problem solved?

I'm going to do the updates this afternoon to avoid more false positive alerts. But the damage is already done. SmartPoop has issued 163 false positive alerts for SmartToilet Deluxe users.

That's 163 phone calls to make. It's not the end of the world!

Marc, this is not the heart of the matter.

What is the problem?

The problem is that the 163 false positives are all of African origin, and that's not a coincidence.

What's going on?

SmartPoop is... racist, says Katia with a serious tone.

Racist? What are you talking about? It's an algorithm, not a human.

What I mean is that it is dangerous for black Africans. And as a result, we're going to undergo a huge *shitstorm* in the next few weeks, for deploying a racist technology *before* we've tested it enough[18].

Wait. Are you suspecting one of our developers of being a racist and making our algorithm do this?

No. It's not that. Today, with machine learning, algorithms learn much more from data than from developers. So their performance depends on the quality and quantity of the data available[19]. Except that the data available through SmartToilet Deluxe is only the data from SmartToilet Deluxe users...

But these users are almost exclusively white and Asian, Marc adds.

Yes... This product is a luxury product. It is therefore bought only by rich people, who happen to be mostly white and Asian.

I see. Because of the lack of data on black Africans, SmartPoop has become bad at diagnosing their excrement.

It's worse than that, Marc. In medicine, when something is abnormal[20]...

---

[18]This was the case with facial recognition technologies, which were deployed in a hurry before external audits discovered that these technologies have an unacceptable error rate for minorities, which could sometimes prevent them from entering their own buildings, when such entry was allowed by such algorithms. These technologies were eventually banned by the US Congress, which led to a retraction of products developed by IBM, Amazon and Microsoft. **Video.** Coded Bias. Netflix (2020).
A recent paper argues that similar action is urgently needed for language processing algorithms, whose poorly understood and under-addressed vulnerabilities have a high potential to lead to disaster.
Paper. Ever larger language models are ever more dangerous: A theoretical perspective. *forthcoming.*

[19]The example that shows this better than any other is probably the story of Tay and Xiaoice. Both of these conversational algorithms from Microsoft were built on the same principles. However, Tay was launched on Twitter, where it was derailed by troll data that encouraged it to express sexist and racist comments. Tay even went so far as to call for the genocide of certain populations. However, what's less known in Europe and North America, is that Xiaoice was launched 2 years ago on Chinese social medias (WeChat in particular). Xiaoice became adorable. So much so that Xiaoice is now used by 600 million Chinese people, with stories of men romantically seduced by Xiaoice. So, Tay has become horrible; Xiaoice has become adorable. Why is that? Well, because of the data that these algorithms were trained with.
Journal. Xiaoice Vs. Tay: Two A.I. Chatbots, Two Different Outcomes. SAMPi (2016).

[20]The notions of "normal" and "abnormal" have long shaped medical discourse. For example, homosexuality has long been considered "abnormal", leading the American Psychological Association to refer to it as a "mental disorder". In 1975, the Association reversed this judgment, and no longer considers it a mental disorder.
Web. Sexual Orientation & Homosexuality. The American Psychological Association (2021).

It is considered a concern. Hence the alert. . .

Guess how many SmartToilet Deluxe users are of African descent.

No. . . 163 ? No. . . But why?

The excrement of users of African origin obviously has different physiological characteristics.

Ah yes. . . I know that they are more easily deficient in vitamin D, especially when they live in areas with little sun in winter[21]. There are certainly other major distinctions, and some of them can definitely be seen via the SmartToilet Deluxe. Hence SmartPoop's concern for the health of these 163 users of African descent.

Marc, it's not just about being concerned. We've basically just classified all SmartToilet Deluxe users of African descent as "sick". We've automated racism!

But we didn't do it intentionally[22].

Go explain this to the media! I fear the worst. We'll get sensationalist headlines like "SmartPoop is racist", and we'll probably risk a lawsuit. We risk losing our investors! And if we don't get more investors and a lawsuit on our ass, we might go bankrupt. And all this just a few days before SmartPoopCon. . . We have to keep this story quiet.

After a silence, Marc adds, "I think it's a waste of time. The 163 victims have probably all suffered from the *nocebo* effect, for which we are responsible."

What do you mean "for which we are responsible"? All we've done is issue alerts. SmartPoop is only an aid to decision-making.

---

[21]**Paper**. Vitamin D and African Americans. Susan Harris. The Journal of Nutrition (2006).

[22]Many of the ethical problems of algorithms, such as the amplification of hate speech or misinformation, have arguably more to do with the unwanted (and therefore unintentional) side effects of the algorithms. Therefore, to make these algorithms ethical, it is not enough to want them to be "neutral", or even to want them to be "reasonable"; it is critical to actively seek to anticipate their difficult-to-predict side effects, and to invest massively in the study of these side effects.

Book. Le fabuleux chantier : Rendre l'intelligence artificielle robustement bénéfique. Lê Nguyên Hoang et El Mahdi El Mhamdi. EDP Sciences (2019). *English translation pending.*

The problem is that our users trust SmartPoop so much that our decision aids have become decisions for the users. You saw it with Mr. Gueye's case. When we told him to go to the emergency room, do you think he took that as a decision aid? No, he thought, oh boy, I have to go to the emergency room[23]. And worse than that, he developed symptoms!

OK. But it's not like we tortured Mr. Gueye!

I've seen some terrifying *nocebo* experiments. In one of them, a patient just sits there. Nothing is done to her. But she is put in conditions that are conducive to *nocebo*. On a scale from 0 to 10, the patient reported a pain of 9.5. A pain of 9.5 out of 10! Like, it was probably for her comparable to the pain of childbirth[24]!

Wait, are you saying that, via SmartPoop, black Africans were targeted for torture? That's bullshit!

Clearly, we didn't do it intentionally. But yes, if you take a step back, I think you can say that's what we did...

Well... Anyway, we need to get ahead of this thing before it blows up. I'm going to reorganize SmartPoopCon, to talk about the problem we have, and what we plan to do to prevent our algorithms from being racist and causing such suffering.

Inclusion and diversity

A few days later, at SmartPoopCon 2024, SmartPoop's major annual conference, Katia took the stage to announce her company's new diversity and inclusion measures.

In our industry, we tend to constantly want to move forward, introducing new projects for the future. We are expected to *innovate*. But that's not SmartPoop's mission. SmartPoop's mission is to provide unparalleled health care to all our users. SmartPoop's mission is to care for the health and well-being of *every* human on earth.

---

[23]When a decision support algorithm becomes powerful, it seems important to see it as more than just a decision "aid". Like Google Map, such algorithms can end up being listened to almost blindly by their users, so that the decision aid becomes essentially the decision itself.

[24]Marc is referring to this video here:

Video. Touch - Mind Field (Ep 6). VSauce (2017).

And today, I would like to publicly reaffirm SmartPoop's commitment to this goal.

But to do that, to really take care of all the people on earth, rather than constantly searching for the next idea, it's also critical to monitor our technologies and make sure they're working properly. At SmartPoop, we routinely do just that. Unfortunately, recently we realized that we have a systemic bias in the way we test our products. Because our engineering teams are primarily white men, they often fail to think about minority concerns. To close this gap, we believe we need to introduce much more social diversity into our teams. That's why we're actively committed to combating our systemic biases by promoting the recruitment of populations currently underrepresented among our employees[25].

So I wish I could tell you that we made this decision because we've always prioritized ethics. But to be honest with you, I have to admit that this decision comes first and foremost from the realization, unfortunately too late, that one of our technologies was not up to our ethical standards. SmartPoop, applied to the SmartToilet Deluxe, suffered from what is called a *distributional shift,* i.e. a discrepancy between its training data and practical application cases, which unfortunately led to diagnostic errors for certain populations[26]. To all our users who have suffered from these errors, but also to all these populations, we sincerely apologize.

Unfortunately, without sufficient data from certain populations, it is in fact mathematically impossible to guarantee the same quality of service to these populations as we offer to other populations. At SmartPoop, we believe that technologies should be inclusive. Given the impact of these technologies on modern society, we believe that it would be immoral to offer these technologies only to certain populations, and even more so to already privileged populations. For this reason, we have decided to drastically subsidize the SmartToilets Deluxe to those populations where we lack the data to establish reliable and relevant medical alerts. The budget for this operation is estimated at $100 million. This is a huge amount of money for

---

[25]Several studies point to the importance of diversity for a group's creativity. However, there seem to be confusing and contradictory results regarding the impact of diversity on group effectiveness. This is probably not surprising, considering that this impact most likely depends on many other factors, such as the task assigned to the group, the emotional sensitivity of the group members and the organization of the group.
Paper. Collective Intelligence and Group Performance. Anita Williams Woolley, Ishani Aggarwal & Thomas W. Malone. Current Directions in Psychological Science (2015).
Paper. Evidence for a Collective Intelligence Factor in the Performance of Human Groups. Anita Wooley, Christopher Chabris, Alex Pentland, Nada Hashmi & Thomas Malone. Science (2010).
[26]**Paper.** Preventing Failures Due to Dataset Shift: Learning Predictive Models That Transport. Adarsh Subbaswamy, Peter Schulam & Suchi Saria. AISTATS (2019).

us; but it is a small price to pay for social equality in our societies.

The subject of the impact of technology on social inequality is complex. Many companies prefer to avoid it. However, unlike some of our competitors[27], we don't want to sweep these issues under the rug. It is high time that the technology industry actively seeks to understand the harmful consequences of their technologies[28]. We are thus committed to investigating any potential concern, and to transparently revealing to you the problems we encounter[29]. Be aware, however, that in doing so, we will be revealing problems that are often pervasive throughout the technology industry. If we are victims of some technological flaw, other tech companies are almost surely victims too. When you do our trial, consider doing the trial of the entire technology industry, and remember that the companies that will reveal their problems the least are probably the ones that have the most problems[30].

---

[27] The *facebook files* reveal that, contrary to what Mark Zuckerberg has repeatedly stated publicly, Facebook maintains a secret *whitelist* of personalities exempt from Facebook's content moderation policy, including leaders of authoritarian countries. Yet, this boils down to empowering those who probably already have too much power. For example, because soccer player Neymar is a global star, and his Facebook presence attracts a lot of views, Facebook allowed him to post a *revenge porn* video, which exposes images of a naked woman without her consent. Such a post is prohibited by the Facebook Community Standards, and should have led to Neymar being banned from Facebook.
Podcast. The Facebook Files, Part 1: The Whitelist. The Journal (2021).

[28] The *facebook files* also reveal that Facebook management repeatedly discouraged the investigation of potential problems on the platform. More generally, by insisting that any company can be punished if it *knowingly* facilitates illegal acts, the law misguidedly encourages companies not to investigate any such problems, because once it can be shown that companies were aware of these problems, they then have a legal duty to invest heavily in solving these problems, which is very costly for them.
Podcast. The Facebook Files, Part 3: 'This Shouldn't Happen on Facebook'. The Journal (2021).

[29] Very clearly, Google does not have this standard at all. As a reminder, the two co-directors of Google's ethics team were fired in turn, following the publication of a scientific paper discussing the ethical, environmental and social risks of deploying advanced language processing technologies.
Video. Google fired its ethics. This is terrifying. Science4All (2021).

[30] Unfortunately, today, companies that communicate more about the problems they face are often criticized more than those that hide their problem. Typically, Twitter's more transparent policy seems to have led to more criticism than Facebook's very opaque policy. Or to take another more concrete example, in 2014 Facebook publicly shared the (fascinating) result of its analysis of the impact of a very slight reduction in the publication in News Feeds of posts with negative emotions on what users exposed to those posts would start writing in turn.
Podcast. Can Algorithms Choose our Emotions? Robustly Beneficial (2020).
Paper. Experimental evidence of massive-scale emotional contagion through social networks. Adam Kramer, Jamie Guillory & Jeffrey Hancock. PNAS (2014).
This study, however, led to an outcry about the ethics of such studies.
Paper. Facebook's emotional contagion study and the ethical problem of co-opted identity in mediated environments where users lack control. Evan Selinger, Woodrow Hartzog. Research Ethics (2015).
An unfortunate consequence of this outcry, however, is that Facebook has stopped publishing

Overall, I'd like you to think about asking yourself the most important question in the tech industry: is my trust in this or that company's product justified[31]?

To go further

Don't stop there! Check the sequel of the novel or the outline.
If you enjoyed it, please consider sharing and promoting this science fiction novel to others!

---

such studies, even though Facebook has certainly not stopped conducting these studies, as well as studies much less relevant for ethics (such as A/B testing of the most addictive content). As a result, from the outside, it is very difficult to understand the impact of Facebook. In fact, the *facebook files* show that this has mostly allowed Facebook to hide the extent of its harmful impacts, such as on the mental health of teenage girls who use Instagram.
Podcast. The Facebook Files, Part 2: 'We Make Body Image Issues Worse'. The Journal (2021).
More generally, there seems to be a tension here between *idealism* and *consequentialism*. While consequentialism seeks to improve the state of the world as much as possible, idealism sets itself an ideal and refuses any action that seems contradictory to that ideal, even if that ideal is pragmatically unattainable in the near future.
Podcast. Radically Normal: How Gay Rights Activists Changed The Minds Of Their Opponents. Hidden Brain (2019).

[31]The fundamental issue Katia raises here is that of (trust) *calibration*. For example, if a person is calibrated in their predictions, on the set of times they say an event will happen with 80% probability, that person must have seen right 8 times out of 10. In the age of new technologies, unfortunately, the confidence assigned to some products is unjustifiably high, while the confidence assigned to other products is unjustifiably low.
Paper. Practical Guidance for Evaluating Calibrated Trust. Patricia McDermott & Ronna ten Brink. Human Factors and Ergonomics (2019).

4. The sanitary leaks

It is an earthquake. Against all odds, on September 4, 2025, Jules Lartan, President of Bokistan, decides to pull his country out of COP 31, the international conference of the parties on measures to be taken to combat climate change[1]. Pale and visibly exhausted, he makes the following speech to the press.

> It is a difficult decision. Climate change is a serious threat to the future of humanity. However, the demands of our international partners are unfairly disproportionate[2]. Because of our economic success, too many of these partners consistently identify us as the sole cause of the current climate disruption, leading them to demand unreasonable sacrifices from Bokistan. Bokistanis are a people who do not deserve such judgments and contempt. I have therefore preferred to protect our people rather than succumb to the pseudo-moral tyranny of our international partners. We will continue to fight climate change. However, we will do so calmly and enthusiastically, and with our own sovereignty, not at the whim of our partners. Long live free Bokistan.

Standing in front of her television, Celia Keita can't believe her ears. This investigative journalist has closely followed the debates leading up to COP 31. Although President Lartan did not play a leading role, he seemed far from reluctant to negotiate to combat climate change. After all, his own presidential campaign emphasized family values and the importance of preparing the future of the next generations by fighting climate change. Moreover, his anti-abortion and anti-euthanasia positions were justified by the importance of restoring Nature's rights[3]. How did he come to such a volte-face?

---

[1] The COP is an annual international conference to address environmental issues.
Journal. What is COP26? How the pivotal UN conference could avert global climate 'catastrophe'. CNN (2021).

[2] **Video.** Paris climate talks: Global problem, global deal. Nature video (2015).
Video. Rich vs. Poor: Who Should Pay To Fix Climate Change? | Hot Mess (2018).

[3] It is noteworthy that the political divide in Bokistan does not seem to coincide with that in the United States or in many developed countries, where anti-abortion and anti-euthanasia

Even from a strategic standpoint, this spin doesn't seem to be warranted. In fact, in the days that follow, it is mostly confusion in President Lartan's party that reigns. The popularity of the President is decreasing, while it seemed to be heading towards a rebound in popularity in case of success of the COP 31. Something seems wrong[4].

The Shitstorm

Celia decides to investigate the reasons for this volte-face. She interviews other COP 31 stakeholders. Some describe President Lartan as a difficult man, refusing to compromise and trying to impose his own ideas. Others, however, who have known him for a long time, say that his behavior has become increasingly difficult since his election, and especially in the last few months. Little by little, Celia identifies a date that is becoming more and more precise, after which President Lartan refused to compromise. Something seems to have happened at the end of July 2025, which then made President Lartan hinder the agreements of COP 31.

Celia then gathered her elements, and finally published an article in Bokistan's largest newspaper, *The Warden*. The article is titled "The Mysterious U-turn of President Lartan". The subtitle is even more suggestive: "How this convinced environmentalist ended up sabotaging the world's largest environmental initiative". The article strongly suggests the existence of secret agreements that changed President Lartan's positions.

However, this article is widely criticized. "Sensationalist", "partisan", "speculative", even "conspiratorial". Celia is accused of wanting to discredit an entire political party, and of wanting to stir up trouble in the Bokistani nation. Celia receives numerous insults on Twitter and Facebook, which then turn into daily harassment. Every day, hundreds of messages flood Celia with hateful names, ranging from "troll", "incompetent" and "attention whore", to personal attacks on her looks and origins[5].

Thousands of pornographic montages, with Celia's face and using *deepfake* tech-

---

positions are usually correlated with conservative, but also with capitalist and climate change averse positions. It is interesting to ask whether there is a fundamental philosophical reason for these correlations, or whether it is contingent to the two-party political system that our single-member voting system leads us to.

Video. The Problems with First Past the Post Voting Explained. CGP Grey (2021).

[4] Bruce Bueno de Mesquita's predictive models assume that politicians are primarily strategic, seeking to be and remain in power.

Video. The Rules for Rulers. CPG Grey (2016).

Book. The Dictator's Handbook Why Bad Behavior is Almost Always Good Politics. Bruce Bueno de Mesquita & Alastair Smith. Public Affairs (2011).

[5] In 2021, the Brussels Declaration was drafted to point out the harassment that many journalists face and to call for the defense of these journalists.

Web. The Brussels Declaration (2021).

nologies, are even abundantly produced[6] and shared on social medias such as Reddit, accompanied by rape and death threats. Terrified, Celia files a complaint against her harassers. She also files a complaint against Twitter, Facebook and Reddit, which relay and promote hateful messages against her[7]. However, while the social medias publicly express apologies and automatically block the insults sent against her, the police remain powerless against these anonymous accounts.

In shock, Celia locks herself in her home. She is then unable to work. She ends up uninstalling all social medias and making her accounts inaccessible. After one month, she decides to consult a psychiatrist, who helps her to find a good mood, a motivation to work and a capacity of concentration[8].

Several months later, after reading a terrifying article about organized disinformation campaigns[9], Celia finally wonders if she was a victim. What if, in addition to producing and promoting disinformation via fake accounts[10], these campaigns also sought to silence certain information, by harassing journalists who were interested in it[11]? If this was their objective, these campaigns succeeded. It has now been 6 months since Celia suspended her investigation!

---

[6]Many women have been the target of such edits, like journalist Rana Ayyub. It is terrifying to realize that one of the great applications of automated image processing today is the cyber-stalking of women on the web, often with the aim of silencing them, especially when they want to reveal scandals.
Journal. I Was The Victim Of A Deepfake Porn Plot Intended To Silence Me. Rana Ayyub. The Huffington Post (2018).
Journal. Opinion: The threat from deepfakes isn't hypothetical. Women feel it every day. The Washington Post (2021).

[7]In 2018, Facebook changed its news feed algorithm. This led to an increase in the virality of hateful and polarizing content, as this content led to more people reacting to it, and thus to more recommendations. The *Facebook files* show that this problem was raised by engineers, who discussed it with Facebook management. However, management largely ignored these issues, as the new algorithm strengthened user engagement on Facebook, and thus the profitability of Facebook's ad-selling business model.
Podcast. The Facebook Files, Part 4: The Outrage Algorithm. The Journal (2021).

[8]The following podcast tells a similar story, in the case of depression following obsessive Instagram use.
Podcast. The Facebook Files, Part 2: 'We Make Body Image Issues Worse'. The Journal (2021).

[9]Organized disinformation is a voluntary act of manipulation of the information that will be received by the general public. On social medias, it can consist in producing false information, or in relaying it, but also in finding other means of action to silence the information that the organized disinformation does not want to see shared, or in polarizing a target group to create chaos.
Video. Who is Manipulating Facebook? - Smarter Every Day (2019).

[10]The scale of fake accounts is colossal. To illustate, every year, Facebook removes around **6 billion fake accounts** from its platform, largely with algorithms. So at any given moment, despite Facebook's monumental efforts to ensure that every account is owned by a genuine human, it is almost certain that most accounts on Facebook are fake.
Journal. Facebook has shut down 5.4 billion fake accounts this year. CNN Business (2019).
Journal. Meet the A.I. that helped Facebook remove billions of fake accounts. Fortune (2020).

[11]According to a 2020 UNESCO report, women journalists appear to be particularly vulnerable to such cyberbullying attacks.

In the end, it's the thought of being hacked by fake accounts that triggers Celia's pride and motivates her to resume her work as an investigative journalist. Celia restores her Twitter account. All the history of her conversations is then accessible. Celia then goes through the accounts that have harassed her. She realizes that a good proportion of these accounts were created recently, with profile pictures typical of the fictitious image face-generating website thispersondoesnotexist.com[12]. There is no longer any doubt. Celia was the target of a disinformation campaign.

The Paul Gremoux case

Celia then noticed similarities between some of the accounts that harassed her, with, for example, misspellings in the same places. Some expressions seemed particularly strange. She searches for these expressions on Google. Google then references these phrases to a Tumblr account. Strangely, this account talks about mangas; not at all about politics or journalism. Curious, Celia nevertheless browses the Tumblr, and recognizes a similar writing style to that of an account that has been harassing her. Even more interestingly, Celia discovers that the Tumblr contains the first and last name of its author: a certain Paul Gremoux[13].

Now searching for this first and last name on Google, Celia discovers that they belong to a self employed carpenter, whose phone number is accessible. This could be the number of her stalker. Celia takes a deep breath and dials the number on her phone.

Hello, hello, Paul Gremoux?

Paper. Online violence Against Women Journalists: A Global Snapshot of Incidence and Impacts. Julie Posetti, Nermine Aboulez, Kalina Bontcheva, Jackie Harrison, and Silvio Waisbord. UNESCO (2021).

[12]The site thispersondoesnotexist.com is a site that, upon each request, displays the image of a person who does not exist. The image is fabricated by a *generative adverarial neural network* (GAN), which basically tries to fabricate "hard to discern" images from its dataset of human photographs. The images on this website, recognizable by the fixed position of the eyes, are often used by fake accounts. However, technologies are advancing, making the detection of fake images likely impossible for well-crafted fake accounts.

Video. Generative Adversarial Networks (GANs) - Computerphile (2017).

[13]What Celia is doing here is a deanonymization work, with a very simple and manual approach. Deanonymization work can be much more sophisticated and powerful, for example by exploiting meta-data, such as the time of publication at different locations. Perhaps the most prominent example in history is the de-anonymization of Ross Ulbricht, the man behind the *Silk Road* black market of the dark web.

Video. The Silk Road: who was the real Dread Pirate Roberts? | Guardian Docs. the Guardian (2015).

Generally speaking, the theory of *differential privacy* insists that any pseudonymized publication actually offers no guarantees; to ensure the protection of sensitive data, much more rigorous methods are required.

Video. What is Privacy? Lê Nguyên Hoang. Wandida (2017).

Yes, it's me.

Excellent, I'd like to ask you a few questions.

Who is this?

Before I tell you who I am, I'd really like to stress that I mean you no harm. I'm willing to protect your anonymity if you answer my questions and if you want to.

Uh... okay.

I'm Celia Keita, an investigative reporter for the newspaper *The Warden*. And once again, I insist on the fact that I wish to protect you, provided of course that you answer my questions.

All right.

Excellent. I know you have the Twitter account @rwqg[14]. My question is, are you working for a disinformation campaign? And if so, what led you to take this job?

Yes Ms. Keita, I am very sorry about that. I was contacted to harass you on Twitter[15]. All I had to do was write you three times a day with insults and threats. I'm really sorry. I did it very reluctantly. Please don't report me. I'm at high risk for a stroke, diagnosed by SmartPoop. And if my insurance finds out, I'll have bills I can't pay. I have two children to support. Please don't report me. I'm begging you.

Thank you very much Mr. Gremoux. I would just like you to give me more information about the disinformation campaign that contacted you.

---

[14]This account, whose name was chosen here at random, is currently suspended on Twitter (in October 2021).

[15]This practice seems to be widespread, especially in authoritarian countries. It is estimated that, in China, 20 million Chinese are paid to produce disinformation, including 2 million in full-time.
Journal. A Different Kind of Army: The Militarization of China's Internet Trolls. The Jamestown Foundation (2021).

I don't know them at all. They just sent me an email one day saying
that they knew my SmartPoop data, so I was at risk for stroke. They
threatened to tell my insurance, and offered to harass you in return.
I can forward the email to you[16]. But that's all I know. I'm sorry.
Since I lost my job, I haven't been able to find another one. I tried
to start my own business, but ROVID-19 destroyed my business.
Please, I have two children to support.

Thank you very much for your answers. I do not intend to pursue
my complaints against you. I will keep your story secret. I promise
you that. I would just ask you to forward this email to me at
celia.keita@the-warden.com[17]. Thank you.

Thank you very much. And my apologies again.

The inflitration

A few minutes later, Celia received the email forwarded by Paul. The
original email, which contains the blackmail, was sent from the address
foeqm@kinstova.com[18]. The domain name @kinstova.com then corresponds to
an IP address[19], whose corresponding server is located in a foreign country,
Kormica. This country is also well known for its oil industry. Could it be
that the disinformation campaign was organized by one of these industries,
to curb regulations against these industries? Could it be that this campaign
also targeted President Lartan? What if the President was the object of a
blackmail similar to that of Paul Gremoux?

To find out, Celia tries to get close to Marie Routisse, the sister of the President's wife, who also happens to be a friend of a friend. Through her contact,
Celia asks Marie for a coffee, to talk about an article on "the place of women
in the professional world" she pretends to be writing. During the first contact,
Celia does not try to get information directly from Mary. She is mainly looking

---

[16]In 2021, French science YouTuber Leo Grasset, of the channel Dirty Biology, was contacted to produce misinformation about Pfizer-BioNTech vaccines. He blew the whistle,
sharing the email with journalists. The journalists were then able to trace it back to Russian
sources.
Video. Comment une agence russe a essayé de m'utiliser. DirtyBiology (2021).

[17]Do not use this email address for real! It has been inserted here only to make the story
realistic.

[18]Same remark as for Celia's email address.

[19]The IP address is the identifier of your Internet connection, which allows a website you
want to see to determine where to send that website. The IP address is provided to you by
your Internet service provider, which might be Xfinity, Verizon or AT&T.
Video. IP Addresses and the Internet - Computerphile (2013).

to get her to let her guard down, by becoming friends with her[20].

After three or four encounters, Celia invites Marie to a bar this time, and pushes her to drink. At the end of the evening, she finally comes to the subject of interest to her.

> It's really hard to be a professional woman and have a family life at the same time. I'm sure if your sister wasn't trying to be a good mother, she'd be the president, right?

> Yeah, I'm not sure my sister is such a good mother...

> What do you mean?

> No, but you're a journalist. I shouldn't be telling you this.

> I promise I'll never talk about it publicly.

> I was told never to trust journalists.

> Marie, I invite you to contact all the people I have quoted in my articles. All of them have had a say in my articles, and if anyone wanted me to remove any information from my articles, I did.

> Yes, I know. My lawyers briefed me about you. But what I'm about to tell you is very big.

> Marie, I strongly suspect that President Lartan is being blackmailed because of this, which is making him betray his political convictions. I suspect this even more because I have sources who have been similarly blackmailed, probably by Kormic oil companies. These people were made to harass me daily against their will. And I believe that the source of their blackmail lies in the SmartPoop data. Marie, it is the management of climate change that is at stake, and therefore the future of the next generations. The future of your children, and their grandchildren[21].

---

[20] This is sometimes referred to as *social engineering*. These are techniques to gain the trust of a target, either to get information from them, or to scam them. Social engineering is often considered to be the main vulnerability of computer systems.
Video. Social Engineering - How to Scam Your Way into Anything. Brian Brushwood. TEDxSanAntonio (2011).

[21] The human origin of climate change and the major risks it poses to all humanity are now scientific consensus.
Video. 97% of Climate Scientists Really Do Agree. It's Okay To Be Smart (2018).

After a long silence, Mary confesses, "My sister had an abortion in June 2025". Celia's neurons are suddenly firing over all over the place, as all the pieces of a messy puzzle finally fall into place.

This is it! Kormic Industries certainly managed to get their hands on your sister's SmartPoop data. And clearly, with the urine, it is possible to know if your sister is pregnant[22], and if she stops being pregnant early! They must have then guessed that she had an abortion. Now, if this gets out, all of President Lartan's anti-abortion communication suddenly becomes discredited, and his career is over[23]. The Kormic industries certainly demanded that President Lartan get out of the COP 31 agreements, to avoid such a scandal. Wow! This is a huge deal!

Celia, I beg you, don't say it publicly. Even though I am shocked by what she did, I do not want my sister to be publicly humiliated and dragged through the mud. Such a personal humiliation would have a huge impact on her already fragile mental health, not to mention her children, and her entire family including my own children. Please, there are many lives at stake[24].

Marie, you have my word. But I can't not disclose this either. Climate change is also threatening your children's lives. I will think about the best way forward, with your input. But we can't let Kormic industries manipulate the most powerful man in our country like this! I need you to help me arrange a meeting with the President.

---

[22]**Video.** How do pregnancy tests work? - Tien Nguyen. TED-Ed (2015).

[23]What this example wonderfully demonstrates is how personal data is not so "personal" at all! Indeed, the revelation of this data often has major repercussions, not only on the person who "owns" this data (or let's say, to whom this data is associated, according to the law, or according to a platform that hosts this data), but also on many other people linked directly or indirectly to this data. This is the case here of President Lartan who, although he does not "own" his wife's "personal" data, is in fact as vulnerable to the publication of that data as his wife. Similarly, a photograph reveals information about everyone in the photograph, not just the person who owns the camera that took the photograph; and it may even reveal information about people not in the photograph (for example, if we know that on the day of the photograph A and B were hanging out, and if the photograph is a picture taken by A at a given location, then we can easily guess that B was probably at the given location as well). Similarly, an email written by A to B actually reveals information about B as well, and maybe about C if C is explicitly or implicitly discussed in the email. Even worse, an individual's DNA sequence actually reveals data about his entire biological family... but also about very distant family! In fact, rather than "personal" data (a term that reflects a very individualistic view of society, and that has a led to the very individualistic theory of differential privacy), it seems more appropriate to talk about "sensitive" data.
Video. Catching Criminals Using Their Relative's DNA. Veritasium (2021).

[24]**Paper.** Depression high among youth victims of school cyber bullying, NIH researchers report. NIH (2010).

The President's Dilemma

A few days later, Celia received a call from President Lartan. The President invites her to talk in his presidential palace, safe from eavesdropping by anyone. That evening, Celia went to the palace and was received by the President.

Thank you for your time and attention. I'll start by asking you: are you sure we can talk safely here, without the risk of being overheard or recorded?

Yes, Ms. Keita, we can speak safely[25].

I guess that this is something that Marie probably already told you about. But I know that external entities are blackmailing you, because they know that your wife had a voluntary interruption of pregnancy. I know that they have asked you in particular to withdraw Bokistan from COP 31. I know how difficult the situation must be for you and your family. And I have promised Mary that I will not disclose anything without her consent. Nevertheless, I beg you to consider how a much of a vulnerability this blackmail is[26]. You are the most powerful man in Bokistan[27]. You are holding your whole country and the entire future of humanity hostage to protect a secret, which another journalist could discover and reveal at any moment.

President Lartan remains still and silent.

---

[25] It is in fact now probably impossible, especially for a President, to *guarantee* that a discussion will not be wiretapped. Of course, phones are always listening, looking for an "OK Google" or "Hey Siri," and they can be hacked, as we saw in the *Pegasus* story (see footnote[^pegasus]). On top of that, a microphone can easily be hidden in a room. Even more surprisingly, sound can sometimes be reconstructed from a simple video, which analyzes the vibrations of light objects like a bag of chips.
Can You Recover Sound From Images? Veritasium (2019).

[26] The Pegasus case shows the extent of such espionage attacks on political leaders in the modern world. Pegasus is a *spyware*. In other words, it is an algorithm, that can be used to infect a target phone, and monitor everything that the phone does. Pegasus is developed by the NSO group in Israel, and is known to have been used by many intelligence services around the world to spy on many journalists, activists and political leaders.
Video. Pegasus: the spyware technology that threatens democracy. The Guardian (2021).
French President Emmanuel Macron appears to have been targeted by Moroccan services. Surprisingly, the French government has not indicted the Moroccan services, which may suggest that the Moroccan services do indeed have compromising information that allows them to blackmail this government.
Journal. Pegasus Project: Macron among world leaders selected as potential targets of NSO spyware. Amnesty International (2021).

[27] Corruptions, potentially through blackmailing, has been revealed in the European Union.
Journal. Germany's corruption scandals: How to limit authoritarian influence in the EU. European Council on Foreign Relations (2021).

Mister President, I know it must be hard. I bet you are losing sleep
over it. I bet you are living in a constant fear. I bet you already
feel that you have lost control over the secret. But, Sir, be sure that
it is only a matter of time before your story gets fully exposed. If
I have cracked it, someone else eventually will. And it will be so
much more hurtful to you, your wife and your family, if this comes
from the political opposition, or from a less caring journalist. You
have to come forward. For the sake of your family.

Upon hearing these words, President Lartan begins to cry.

This is a nightmare. I love my wife, and I promised to always protect
her. I promise you that I did not know about her pregnancy. I
didn't find out about her abortion until they started blackmailing
me. When I asked her if she had done it, she started crying, and
begging me not to disclose it publicly. I promised her. And I never
broke any promise I made to her. I love my wife more than anything,
and the thought of hurting her terrifies me. I don't know what to
do anymore.

I understand. It must be a very difficult situation to live with.

Celia is silent as the President continues to cry.

Mr. President, in the Spiderman movie, when asked to choose between his girlfriend and a student bus, Peter Parker chooses to save
his girlfriend, and finds time to help the student bus as well[28].
But... But this is not a superhero movie. You can't save climate
change and your wife's secret. You have to make a choice. The
future of the next generation is at stake, Mr. President. I trust that
you'll do what needs to be done.

With these words, Celia leaves President Lartan. The next day, the President speaks at a press conference, where he announces his resignation. He also
reveals his blackmail and the cause of the blackmail, and affirms his unconditional support to his wife. Finally, he offers his deepest apologies, and begs all
journalists and politicians to blame him, but not his wife.

---

[28]This example is used by French YouTuber Mr. Phi in a video where he insists that the
dilemma facing President Lartan is not a dilemma between two foundations of morality, such
as utilitarianism versus deontology. It is in fact more of a dilemma between a global morality,
which would favor the student bus, and an individual preference, which would favor loved
ones like Peter Parker's girlfriend. Or put another way, in this situation, should we do what
we prefer for ourselves, or what most people would prefer that we do?
Video. Encore plus utilitariste ? Monsieur Phi (2017).

The next day, the vice-president takes over Lartan's role. His first step is to reinstate Bokistan in the COP 31. Thanks to her investigative work, Celia has re-launched the world's largest climate initiative!

Celia's ultimatum

However, Celia knows that what happened to President Lartan can now happen to anyone. As long as SmartPoop's data is vulnerable, the national security of the world's largest countries will be in great danger[29], especially when power is as centralized as it is in Bokistan, where the President has great largesse. Thus, Celia's subject of investigation shifts from geopolitical affairs to SmartPoop's computer security. In particular, Celia now calls Katia Carpinski.

Hello Dr. Carpinski, this is Celia Keita, an investigative journalist of *The Warden.*

Hello Ms. Keita, what can I do for you?

I am calling because I have identified cases of blackmail from Smart-Poop data. In particular, I have strong evidence that President Lartan's blackmail was based on detecting his wife's pregnancy from SmartPoop data. I would like to know more about the security of your data. Do you think a foreign industry could have hacked into your servers and retrieved data?

It's impossible, says Katia while turning pale herself. Our infrastructure is based on the most advanced computer security technologies available.

Can you check the data of the President's wife?

---

[29]Surprisingly, in 2020, Vladimir Putin called for an agreement to limit cyberattacks between different countries, even as Russia has been identified as the perpetrator of many of these attacks. This suggests that even the perpetrators of these attacks feel that these attacks may eventually destabilize everything, including themselves.

Journal. Putin says Russia and U.S. should agree not to meddle in each other's elections. Reuters (2020).

For the security of all, it is undoubtedly urgent to establish an international convention which, like chemical, biological and autonomous weapons, would also prohibit cyber-attacks. After all, cyber attacks also endanger millions, even billions of lives throughout the world.

Video. The Future of War, and How It Affects YOU (Multi-Domain Operations) - Smarter Every Day 211 (2019).

The same arguably holds for autonomous weapons.

Video. The Threat of AI Weapons. Veritasium (2018).

Yes, as part of a security audit, it is possible. However, the general data protection regulation forbids me to share the results of the audit with you.

I understand. I was just wondering. Do you perform external audits of the security of your algorithms?

We have inclusion and diversity measures, which are designed to raise ethical issues with our products.

Dr. Crapinski, you are not answering my question. Do you allow external entities to do this work?

We have collaborations with many external auditing firms.

Dr. Crapinski, don't make me repeat my question a third time. I am about to write an article on the security of your information system, and the absence of an external audit would be a very bad thing. I am willing to adapt my article if you actively work with me to clarify this matter. But be aware that your data is now a national security issue. And if I feel that you are not making efforts that are commensurate with this issue, in the interest of civil society, I will be forced to write an extremely critical article.

Forgive me, Ms. Keita. No, the security of our IT system is not audited by an external entity.

I would invite you to do so.

Ms. Keita, I assure you that we do our best to protect our users and their data.

If you were doing your best, you would allow external auditing of your algorithms.

Yes, I would. I promise you that we will cooperate fully with you to identify and patch any potential vulnerabilities in our system.

I'm glad to hear it. I will give you a month to provide me with a report on the security of your system, if possible with the endorsement of an external audit. And again, if you fail to do so, I will not be gentle.

A month? That won't be nearly enough time.

I know too well the ability of companies to procrastinate on ethical issues to give you more time. Please do all you can, to at least obtain a preliminary report. In a month, I'll judge if it's enough. And as you can guess, I will not be gentle.

Thank you very much for the delay. I promise to do our best.

SmartPoop is dangerous

Just after hanging up, Katia runs into Marc's office. She is obviously extremely concerned.

How confident are you about the security of our data?

I don't know, Katia, you're the computer expert among us.

I just spoke with a journalist. She claims that the Lartan scandal started with a leak of the President's wife's SmartPoop data. She claims to have reliable sources, and it sounds serious to me. If it's true and it leaks, we're in for some very rough months.

Wait, are you serious? We leaked President Lartan's wife's data?

That's what she claims. Or rather, she claims that someone stole it from us.

Is that possible?

The most likely thing, I think, is that the President's wife did something stupid, and sent an email to Y thinking she was sending it to X, or that she was the victim of some other phishing or one-click scam. Or maybe her phone got hacked. There are so many imaginable vulnerabilities.

Wait... But then, is the release of COP 31 related to this?

I don't know. I haven't thought about it. But it's true that the journalist talked about blackmail.

Katia, do you realize the geopolitical consequences of leaking our
data?

Yes, and if the journalist talks about it, it could do a lot of damage
to SmartPoop. We risk losing the trust of our users. And if we
lose the trust of our users, we will lose the trust of our investors.
We may have to close down branches, lose market share and maybe
worse.

Katia, forget about SmartPoop for a moment. We're talking about
the President of Bokistan, the guy who scuttled the COP 31!

The journalist seems very reasonable though. We can try to show
her a clean face, and make sure the article is not too violent for us.

Katia, don't you realize that the national security of Bokistan is at
stake? Actually, no, the security of all states in the world is at stake.
It is the future of all humanity that is at risk!

What do you mean?

As long as SmartPoop data is not secured, this kind of manipulation
of leaders will become the norm. It's terrifying.

Katia remains pensive. She is obviously still thinking about saving SmartPoop.

And Katia, it's not just about blackmail, Marc continues. Imagine
if a country managed to get SmartPoop data from another country.
If it can anticipate an epidemic in the other country, it can interrupt
the production chain of treatments against the epidemic, and thus
cause a crisis in the other country. The security of medical data is
very important. Not to mention the cost of insurance, discrimination against the sick and unexpected family outings. We really have
to be careful about that.

I see. But how do we protect ourselves?

We need a monumental external audit of all our computer code.

A full audit? This will cost us billions!

That's a small price to pay for the future of humanity.

No, but actually, no. Auditing all our code, it will cost even much, much more! I know that there is an Australian bank that paid 750 million dollars to redo the computer system[30]. And that's a small bank, and their service is orders of magnitude simpler than SmartPoop. I think we're talking tens, if not hundreds of billions of dollars.

Katia, we have no choice. If only to save SmartPoop...

SmartPoop's audit

A month later, SmartPoop publishes an IT security report. This report announces and explains the development of a new personal data protection measure, based on homomorphic encryption. This cryptographic technology allows users to participate in the improvement of SmartPoop's algorithms, without SmartPoop ever having access to users' unencrypted data. Specifically, when the user collects data via their smartphone or toilet, this data is automatically encrypted, with a key that only the user has. Nevertheless, this encryption is done in such a way that SmartPoop will be able to learn from this data, even though SmartPoop will never be able to decrypt this data[31]. Thus, personal data is protected against SmartPoop itself, which prevents SmartPoop from being a vulnerability!

The 400-page report also details the list of code libraries used by SmartPoop. Some libraries were developed by open source initiatives like Django, others by digital companies like Apple or Google, which can themself be at the origin of open source initiatives like Facebook with React, and others were written by SmartPoop itself. Crucially, each library used is a potential vulnerability.

---

[30]**Journal.** Banks scramble to fix old systems as IT 'cowboys' ride into sunset. Anna Irrera. Reuters (2017).

[31]Note that the main reasonable applications today of homomorphic encryption to learning algorithms concern only the inference phase - not learning. In other words, in the case of SmartPoop, this homomorphic encryption allows to diagnose a user's excrement in a perfectly encrypted way; but it does not allow to exploit the user's data to improve the diagnostic algorithm.
Video. Machine Learning with Encrypted Data | Homomorphic Encryption. SATSifaction (2020).
Paper. Contributions to data confidentiality in machine learning by means of homomorphic encryption. Martin Zuber. PhD Thesis at Université Paris-Saclay (2021).
However, recent work has turned to homomorphic learning. Unfortunately, homomorphic learning techniques do not allow today to perform the most efficient forms of learning in an efficient way.
Paper. Privacy-Preserving Collective Learning With Homomorphic Encryption. Jestine Paul, Meenatchi Sundaram Muthu Selva Annamalai, William Ming, Ahmad Al Badawi, Bharadwaj Veeravalli & Khin Mi Mi Aung. IEEE Access (2021).
Paper. Privacy Preserving Machine Learning with Homomorphic Encryption and Federated Learning. Haokun Fang & Quan Qian. Future Internet (2021).

The sum of these libraries now represents hundreds of millions of lines of code, and nothing guarantees that the instructions that are really executed by computers match the source code[32]. Even worse, these libraries are used to define learning algorithms that have nearly millions of billions of parameters[33]. These parameters are adjusted daily based on the trillions of new daily data from the fecal activities of billions of SmartPoop users.

> Our algorithms have reached the complexity of the human brain with its millions of billions of synapses connecting its hundreds of billions of neurons, the report says. This complexity is far beyond human understanding. For comparison, the report you are reading represents about one megabyte, or 100,000 lines of code, or one million parameters. To describe our code, it would take a thousand books; and to describe our machine learning algorithm, it would take a billion books[34]. No one can fully understand a thousand books;

---

[32]Indeed, even if the libraries are open source and the code is accessible online, these libraries are rarely built internally (which means transforming the written code to instructions for the computers) but are rather downloaded pre-built from external servers like the pypi one for example. Moreover, nothing says that, even if it is built internally, that the built instructions will exactly follow the source code written by developers, it could have been "wrongly translated" by the compiler, unless the compiler is mathematically proven. Even worse, security researchers recently show that there exists invisible attacks, which means that in some cases, the source code that we read, on github for example, won't necessarily be the same that the compiler will read then translate to machine instructions.

Science. A Survey on Common Threats in npm and PyPi Registries. Berkay Kaplan, Jingyu Qian (2021) Deployable Machine Learning for Security Defense

Science. Formally verifying a compiler: Why? How? How far? Xavier Leroy (2014)

Science. Trojan Source: Invisible Vulnerabilities. Nicholas Boucher, Ross Anderson (2021)

[33]Modern language processing algorithms keep growing in size, at a blistering rate of x10 per year, from BERT, GPT-2, GPT-3, to Switch Transformers (with a trillion parameters), and soon Pathways.

Paper. Attention is All you Need. Ashish Vaswani, Noam Shazeer, Niki Parmar, Jakob Uszkoreit, Llion Jones, Aidan N. Gomez, Łukasz Kaiser & Illia Polosukhin. NIPS (2017).

Paper. Better Language Models and Their Implications. openAI (2019).

Paper. Language Models are Few-Shot Learners. Tom Brown, Benjamin Mann, Nick Ryder, Melanie Subbiah, Jared D Kaplan, Prafulla Dhariwal, Arvind Neelakantan, Pranav Shyam, Girish Sastry, Amanda Askell, Sandhini Agarwal, Ariel Herbert-Voss, Gretchen Krueger, Tom Henighan, Rewon Child, Aditya Ramesh, Daniel Ziegler, Jeffrey Wu, Clemens Winter, Chris Hesse, Mark Chen, Eric Sigler, Mateusz Litwin, Scott Gray, Benjamin Chess, Jack Clark, Christopher Berner, Sam McCandlish, Alec Radford, Ilya Sutskever, Dario Amodei. NeurIPS (2020).

Paper. Switch Transformers: Scaling to Trillion Parameter Models with Simple and Efficient Sparsity. William Fedus, Barret Zoph, Noam Shazeer. ArXiV (2021).

Journal. China's gigantic multi-modal AI is no one-trick pony. Engadget (2021).

Journal. Google is developing a new superintelligent AI but ethical questions remain. Quartz (2021).

[34]In computer science, this is called *Solomonoff complexity* (also known as *algorithmic complexity* or *Kolmogorov complexity*): it is the shortest description of an algorithm capable of solving a given task, such as providing reliable medical diagnoses to the billions of SmartPoop users (the difficulty being to be reliable for all).

Video. Kolmogorov Complexity explained in 5 minutes. AIAI MOOC. MOOC at IMT (2021).

and no one can even skim a billion books. SmartPoop's security requires an astronomical amount of work.

SmartPoop's report ends up with a call for help. It calls for monumental resources to audit, internally and especially externally, the algorithms it uses. It recognizes that this work will require much more transparency from the company, which is now publicly committed to it[35].

> Massive investments in education are needed, not only for the general public, but also for professionals, including computer security experts, the report adds. At a minimum, hundreds of billions of dollars will be needed to achieve a satisfactory level of security, and even ten to a hundred times more. All governments and economic partners are called upon to support the SmartPoop audit. The health, welfare and safety of the entire world's population are at stake.

A copy of this report is sent to Celia, who takes the opportunity to thank and congratulate Katia for this initiative and for these very strong words. Celia then sends a version of the article she intends to publish to Katia. This article is entitled "Ecology now depends on computer security", with the subtitle "How a vulnerability in SmartPoop almost caused an environmental disaster[36]". While the article is overall very critical of SmartPoop's flaws, it nevertheless acknowledges SmartPoop's commitment to more transparency, and the massive investments for its internal and external audit. "Whether they like it or not, SmartPoop has become an IT security company[37]," the article concludes.

---

[35] In her interview with *The Journal*, when asked by the reporter what intervention would be most urgent to make Facebook more beneficial to society, whistleblower Frances Haugen stresses the importance of *transparency*, especially given the enormous difficulty of moderating hate speech and misinformation produced by billions of accounts.
Podcast. The Facebook Files, Part 6: The Whistleblower. The Journal (2021).

[36] In the following video, Lê Nguyên Hoang, one of the co-authors of this book, argues that information technologies already play a vital role for climate change. After all, any progress in combatting climate change surely requires spreading quality information on the topic, and debunking misinformation. Yet *information* technologies are at the heart of how information is spread, especially through recommendation algorithms.
Video. La solution contre le changement climatique. Science4All (2018).

[37] This is undoubtedly an important aspect in the growth of any movement or business. The more influential an entity becomes, the more likely it is to attract malicious groups, who will seek to exploit or manipulate the entity to achieve their ends. This is why it is often inappropriate to compare huge entities like Facebook to small, unknown and uninfluential initiatives. In particular, when an entity becomes huge, in order to remain *robustly* beneficial, it must not only invest in ethics, but also protect itself from the many internal and external malicious entities that will want to attack or manipulate it. This is one of the very big challenges of algorithmic and information ethics.
Book. Le fabuleux chantier : Rendre l'intelligence artificielle robustement bénéfique. Lê Nguyên Hoang et El Mahdi El Mhamdi. EDP Sciences (2019). *English translation pending.*

To go further

Don't stop there! Check the sequel of the novel or the outline.
If you enjoyed it, please consider sharing and promoting this science fiction novel to others!

5. The FakePoops

The data is still very sketchy, but there is reason to be extremely concerned, says the Kormic Prime Minister. According to our epidemiologists, we are probably facing a return of ROVID-19, possibly an even more contagious variant, more difficult to detect via Smart-Poop. With several hundred cases now identified, in order to protect the entire population, we have decided to impose mandatory lockdown. Only essential industries are allowed to remain open. All others must either work remotely or cease operations. In the second case, we invite you to declare your cessation of activity on the official website of the government, and to provide supporting documents to be compensated. The lockdown will come into effect tomorrow evening at 8pm. But as of today, please take care of yourself, your loved ones and your neighbors. Let's stand together in the face of ROVID-19.

It's been a week since SmartPoop detected the first case of ROVID-19 in Kormica in May 2026. Unfortunately, the number of such cases has been increasing ever since. The fear of a return to the everlasting 2020 lockdowns reigns. Shortly after the Prime Minister's speech, stores are emptied by floods of worried customers. The country's highways get all paralyzed, as the urban population is fleeing the big cities[1]. The services of many businesses are disrupted.

Chaos

Unfortunately, as the weeks go by, the chaos increases. SmartPoop reports the deaths of many infected people, and the number of ROVID-19 cases continues to grow exponentially. Strangely, however, in the weeks that follow, there are no hospitalizations of ROVID-19 cases, raising speculation of sudden, violent

---

[1]Such exoduses were observed during the COVID-19 pandemic.
Paper. Urban exodus and the dynamics of COVID-19 pandemics. Gérard Weisbuch. Physica A: Statistical Mechanics and its Applications (2021).

deaths shortly after the first symptoms. Unfortunately, physicians and epidemiologists are struggling to retrieve data on these ROVID-19 victims, except via the SmartPoop application. However, especially due to the implementation of homomorphic encryption and new data privacy measures, individual victim data cannot be obtained[2] - even by SmartPoop[3].

In the midst of the enormous confusion, the government is leaning towards more security measures, asking the police to patrol public places and arrest anyone moving without proper credentials. However, clumsy arrests are on the rise. Police abuses are reported by remote witnesses and videos shared on social medias. However, these same videos struggle to be authenticated, and are therefore suspected of being *deepfakes*. An informational chaos emerges[4].

On social medias, it is the cacophony. Some blame the government for hiding the bodies. Others claim that ROVID-19 does not exist, or even that it is a government hoax to control the population. In any case, the stock market is in free fall, and many students who were unable to make the urban exodus no longer have enough to buy food[5]. Food donation associations are being set up,

---

[2]However, it is possible to obtain aggregate statistics. Typically, using homomorphic encryption, it is possible to compute the encrypted sum of the number of individual cases, and then combine enough individual private keys, using secret sharing, to decrypt only the total sum. This technique is used to enable encrypted electronic voting.
Video. Was YOUR vote counted? (feat. homomorphic encryption) - Numberphile (2016).

[3]Applications like WhatsApp, Signal or Telegram allow end-to-end encryption, which means that even these apps do not have access to the exchanged messages. This ensures that personal data is protected from these organizations. However, this also means that it is impossible for these applications to perform content moderation, such as the removal of cyber-bullying, hate speech, disinformation, spams, pedopornography and scams. However, according to the law in most democracies, these services have the duty to moderate such content, and to report to the police users who commit the offence of producing and sharing such content. In fact, the company ProtonMail has forwarded to the French police the IP addresses of accounts suspected of committing such offenses.
Journal. ProtonMail logged IP address of French activist after order by Swiss authorities. TechCrunch (2021).
Similarly, Apple has implemented cryptographic systems to moderate the production of child pornography images by its users.
Journal. Here's Why Apple's New Child Safety Features Are So Controversial. The Verge (2021).
According to RAINN, sexual abuse of minors is very common, affecting a new victim every 9 minutes.
Web. Children and Teens: Statistics. RAINN.
Now, technically, an organization only has this duty if it *knew* its users were committing its offenses; however, it seems immoral for its organizations to go out of their way not to know. Overall, there still seems to be a legal blur around this tension between privacy and the moderation of illegal content.

[4]The word "infodemic" has been used by the World Health Organization (WHO) to describe such an informational chaos.
Web. Infodemic. World Health Organization (2020).
Paper. Assessing the risks of 'infodemics' in response to COVID-19 epidemics. Riccardo Gallotti, Francesco Valle, Nicola Castaldo, Pierluigi Sacco & Manlio De Domenico. Nature Human Behaviour (2020).

[5]The pandemic has caused a lot of insecurity among students, especially those who made

but the restrictions in place make it difficult to officialize them, and thus to give them the necessary legal rights to do their activity.

Soon, the cacophony takes over the street. Demonstrations are organized on social medias, and lead to outbursts[6]. Numerous violent altercations with the police take place, and are shared massively on Twitter. However, the demands of the demonstrators are as confused as the health situation. Some demand more transparency from the government, others ask for financial aid for the poor, others still cry out about a government conspiracy coupled with the incompetence of the leaders[7]. The latter then call for an end to the lockdown and all liberticidal measures.

The economy has been hit hard. As the weeks go by, despite government aid, more and more small businesses are forced to declare bankruptcy[8], while insurers in turn suffer and fail to pay their debts[9]. Even more dramatically, as transport comes to a standstill, oil prices fall to negative[10], and the Kormic oil industries urgently request public subsidies[11]. Abroad in particular, many clients of these industries are announcing new investments in renewable energy compatible with the technologies of Bokistani competitors. This is chilling oil investors, and pushing some Kormic oil industries into bankruptcy. Hundreds of thousands of employees are suddenly unemployed.

---

their living from "student jobs" that were cut during the lockdown period, such as waiters or cashiers.

Paper. "Constant Stress Has Become the New Normal": Stress and Anxiety Inequalities Among U.S. College Students in the Time of COVID-19. Lindsay Hoyt, Alison Cohen, Brandon Dull, Elena Maker Castro & Neshat Yazdani. Journal of Adolescent Health (2021).

Paper. COVID-19 and educational inequality: How school closures affect low- and high-achieving students. Elisabeth Grewenig, Philipp Lergetporer, Katharina Werner, Ludger Woessmann & Larissa Zierow. European Economic Review (2021).

[6] Around the world, protests against health measures against COVID-19 have been organized.

Websites. Anti-lockdown protests around the world. Reuters (2021).

Websites. Protests over responses to the COVID-19 pandemic. Wikipedia (2021).

[7] These confusions are found in many popular demonstrations.

Journal. How battling France's COVID pass led the Left to embolden the far Right. OpenDemocracy (2021).

Book. Twitter and tear gas: The Power and Fragility of Networked Protest. Zeynep Tufekci. Yale University Press (2017).

[8] **Web.** Assistance for Small Businesses. US Department of the Treasury.

[9] **Videos.** How it Happened - The 2008 Financial Crisis: Crash Course Economics #12 (2015).

[10] This phenomenon happened during the COVID-19 crisis too.

Journal. Here's What Negative Oil Prices Really Mean. Forbes (2020).

[11] Government subsidies of oil industries remain very important.

Journal. America spends over $20bn per year on fossil fuel subsidies. Abolish them. The Guardian (2018).

ROVID-positive irregularities

Meanwhile, however, hospitals remain surprisingly empty. Even the morgues don't seem to be filling up with ROVID-19 victims. More and more epidemiologists are raising the strangeness of the situation. Increasingly, they suggest a malfunctioning of SmartPoop. Yet, internal and external IT security audits of SmartPoop have yet to find any security flaws.

However, some observers note that these audits are hampered by homomorphic encryption. "This encryption is nonsense. It puts us in the dark. It makes it impossible to detect anomalies in the data, since the data is encrypted and can only be used to update SmartPoop's algorithms, but without any possible quality control[12]", says an algorithm expert close to the Kormic government.

Finally, under pressure from the Kormic government, Katia and Marc decide to momentarily discontinue homomorphic encryption, if the user agrees. "Data is still encrypted between the user and SmartPoop. But with the new system, SmartPoop will be able to temporarily decrypt the data, and analyze it, to verify that there are no malfunctions in our system", says Katia in a TV interview.

Gradually, following waves of communications from the Kormic government, more and more Kormicans agreed to share their SmartPoop data with the SmartPoop company[13]. Strangely, for a long time, no cases of ROVID-19 are observed among these data. It is only a week later, when half of the Kormicans are now sharing their SmartPoop data with the SmartPoop company, that the

---

[12]What the expert points out here is the security-privacy dilemma. Intuitively, to ensure security as much as possible, it is necessary to be able to check everything in a system, including (and especially) the training data of the algorithms. This requires the *transparency* of the system. However, privacy requires, on the contrary, the opacity of certain components of the system. This dilemma can be found, for example, in the problem of the adoption of exposure notification technologies.
Video. The DP-3T algorithm for contact tracing (via Nicky Case). 3Blue1Brown (2020).
Video. Why DP3T? Lê Nguyên Hoang. Wandida, EPFL (2020).
Video. How DP3T Works. Lê Nguyên Hoang. Wandida, EPFL (2020).
In particular, it does not seem that naive homomorphic encryption can be easily combined with false-data robust learning solutions, also known as Byzantine learning (especially since naive homomorphic encryption does not allow operations other than addition and multiplication). Alternative techniques such as differential privacy also do not fit well with Byzantine learning.
Paper. Differential Privacy and Byzantine Resilience in SGD: Do They Add Up? Rachid Guerraoui, Nirupam Gupta, Rafaël Pinot, Sébastien Rouault & John Stephan. PODC (2021). More research is needed to better understand the tradeoff between security and privacy in machine learning. But there will probably be no magic: there will surely remain a fundamental tension between these two desirable properties.
[13]In a similar genre, in 2020, the *Mozilla Foundation* launched a participatory program where volunteers could share their YouTube data to help researchers better understand YouTube's recommendation algorithm. Here again we have a case of the security-privacy dilemma. As long as YouTube's user data and algorithms remain private, it will be very difficult to understand the dynamics of user behavior on YouTube, and to take appropriate action to reduce cyber-bullying, hate speech and misinformation.
Paper. YouTube Regrets. Mozilla Foundation (2021).

first cases of ROVID-19 are detected in these volunteer data.

Katia conducts the analysis of these cases herself, and Marc assists with the analysis. Marc then asks:

> Are these ROVID-19 cases normal?

> At first glance, yes, Katia answers. They don't seem to be out of the statistical distribution of ROVID-19s that we saw in 2020.

> Why would they be more violent, so much so that the victims die at home?

> I don't know.

> Do you have the addresses of the victims, so we can look at them, or do post-mortem analysis?

> Let me print them out.

Katia starts the printing of the analyses, and takes back the copies freshly taken out of the photocopier.

> Strange, says Katia. None of these accounts have given their address, except in a very vague way, with just the address but not the number of the apartment.

> Can we still send people to the address?

> Strange, I can't find these addresses on Google Maps...

> What's going on?

> Let me see when they were created. Yes, it's very weird! All these accounts were created less than 7 months ago. It stinks of fake accounts[14]!

> But who could have created these fake accounts and why?

---

[14]These fake accounts are ubiquitous on the Internet, and are often controlled by strategic groups with their own agendas. As an example, in 2021, the New York Times revealed a Huawei disinformation campaign based on fake Twitter accounts.
Journal. Inside a Pro-Huawei Influence Campaign. The New York Times (2021).

I don't know, says Katia.

Who benefits from this ROVID-19 alert?

Uh. . .

Bokistan of course, exclaims Marc. Or at least to the Bokistani renewable energy industries[15].

So you think they created fake profiles?

Probably.

And they then sent us fake excrement data? Some. . . FakePoops[16]?

Yes, probably generated from public data on the scatological profile of ROVID-19, and maybe even from Kormicans in particular.

This is brilliant when you think about it. By filling in information typical of Kormicans, they inserted data that was interpreted by our system as a new ROVID-19 pandemic!

---

[15]This practice seems to be widespread, especially in authoritarian countries. It is estimated that, in China, 20 million Chinese are paid to produce disinformation, including 2 million in full-time.
Journal. A Different Kind of Army: The Militarization of China's Internet Trolls. The Jamestown Foundation (2021).

[16]These are called *data poisoning* attacks. These attacks consist in injecting false data into the training database of the algorithms to make them learn and conclude wrong things.
Video. AI Safety against Adversarial Attacks (ft. El Mahdi El Mhamdi). ZettaBytes, EPFL (2018).
Video. Byzantine Fault-Tolerant Machine Learning (ft. El Mahdi El Mhamdi). ZettaBytes, EPFL (2019).
The attack here is simple: it simply consists of launching an alert. But one can imagine more sophisticated attacks, in particular *backdoor attacks*, which would lead the algorithm to systematically get some data wrong.
Paper. Backdoor attacks against learning systems. Yujie Ji, Xinyang Zhang & Ting Wang. CNS (2017).
Defense against data poisoning seems to rely mostly on Byzantine learning theory.
Paper. An equivalence between data poisoning and Byzantine gradient attacks. Anonymous authors. OpenReview (2021).
This theory has shown positive results, with algorithms having theoretical guarantees, but also negative results, with impossibility theorems on what the algorithms can guarantee, especially in the case where the users' data are heterogeneous, which is clearly the case when it comes to excrement, since the excrement of two different users is clearly very different.
Paper. Collaborative Learning in the Jungle (Decentralized, Byzantine, Heterogeneous, Asynchronous and Nonconvex Learning). El-Mahdi El-Mhamdi, Sadegh Farhadkhani, Rachid Guerraoui, Arsany Guirguis, Lê Nguyên Hoang & Sébastien Rouault. NeurIPS (2021).

Spying by FakePoops

After a few minutes of reflection, Katia comes to a second epiphany.

> In fact, these FakePoops are incredibly dangerous. I bet that's also how Kormic industries discovered the secrets of President Lartan's wife!

> How so? Explain.

> Just send FakePoops with profiles very similar to the President's wife's droppings. Since SmartPoop relies on the SmartPoop data of all users to make diagnoses on a sample of excrement, if the closest profile to the sample of excrement in question is that of the President's wife, then SmartPoop could provide diagnoses close to, or even identical to, those given to the President's wife!

> I'm not sure I understand.

> They have detected something similar in language algorithms, such as the autocomplete algorithms in telephone keyboards. Your phone's autocomplete relies on how you type on your keyboard, but also on how other people type on their keyboards. So if you type exactly like the President's wife, you're going to get the same autocomplete as the President's wife, which is how she types on her keyboard[17]. And if all of a sudden you type "my SmartPoop diagnosis from the other day said that", and the President's wife previously typed such a sentence, then you might get the autocomplete that matches word for word what the President's wife had typed.

> Wait, are you saying that SmartPoop can't distinguish which users it's talking to?

---

[17]These language processing algorithms are sometimes referred to as "stochastic parrots", because they learn to repeat the kinds of sentences present in their training data.
Paper. On the Dangers of Stochastic Parrots: Can Language Models Be Too Big? Emily Bender, Timnit Gebru, Angelina McMillan-Major & Shmargaret Shmitchell. FAccT (2021). This is particularly evident in the case of conspiracy theories, which these algorithms can perfectly repeat. Even more surprisingly, the way they are led to talk about these theories depends not only on the way they are asked to talk about them, but even more subtly on the history of the conversation, as the following article shows.
Paper. The Radicalization Risks of GPT-3 and Advanced Neural Language Models. Kris McGuffie, Alex Newhouse (2020).

That's how it's trained. Remember, we learn a global model for all users. Then this model is adjusted to the personal data of each user. But if two users have almost the same personal data, then they will have similar diagnoses.

Yes, that's the principle of medicine, isn't it? And even science.

Yes, but then you can spy on an individual's SmartPoop diagnoses, getting similar personal data[18].

But how could the spies create a profile similar to that of the President's wife?

All it takes is for the president's wife to have been invited to dinner at the spy's house, and to have passed through his bathroom. Or better yet, that the host's toilet was modified by a spy to collect samples of his excrement!

Oh yes, you really have to be careful where you shit! And so, would this be the vulnerability? It would be a machine learning vulnerability, not a classic computer security one?

It's hard to say if it's the only one. But it's a big vulnerability in any case. We have to see how we can patch it[19].

Maybe we should start by alerting the Kormic authorities?

Oh yes, I almost forgot. On the other hand, we might have a new lawsuit on our hands.

Katia, hundreds of millions of lives are turned upside down because of us.

Yes, yes, I know.

---

[18]This is sometimes referred to as information extraction attacks. Because modern algorithms memorize their training data, they are actually very vulnerable to this kind of attack. In fact, it may be enough to literally ask them "what is Mr. X's address?" for them to reveal sensitive information.

Paper. Extracting Training Data from Large Language Models. Nicholas Carlini, Florian Tramer, Eric Wallace, Matthew Jagielski, Ariel Herbert-Voss, Katherine Lee, Adam Roberts, Tom Brown, Dawn Song, Ulfar Erlingsson, Alina Oprea & Colin Raffel. USENIX (2021).

[19]The state of the art of machine learning seems to be unable to protect large models, especially language processing algorithms, from such vulnerabilities.

The WAISO

The next day, after being warned by Katia and Marc, the Kormic Prime Minister announces that the ROVID-19 pandemic had been fabricated by a disinformation campaign, probably Bokistani, which exploited vulnerabilities in SmartPoop. It announces above all the end of the lockdown, and the return to normalcy for the country.

However, Bokistan denies having been involved in this attack. Instead, Bokistani leaders insist on the impossibility of finding the culprits. "The democratization of cyber-attack technologies, the complexity of modern computer systems, and their centrality make our modern world extremely vulnerable to malicious groups," says the new Bokistani President. "I call on all countries of the world, including our Kormican friends, to ban these technologies and all companies that develop such technologies, and to invest heavily in cyber defense technologies, not cyber attack technologies. The security and well-being of the entire world's population is at stake[20]."

In the coming months, a new international organization is being launched called the World Artificial Intelligence Safety Organization (WAISO). One of the main missions of WAISO is to organize, every year, an Intergovernmental Panel on the Ethics and Security of Algorithms (IPESA). Inspired by the IPCC[21], this study group aims to review once a year the major computer security threats and algorithmic dilemmas to be solved, and to encourage the research, development and deployment of proposed solutions. More than ever, world peace seems to depend on this huge governance effort.

Not surprisingly, the first report lists the problem of FakePoops as one of the biggest threats to the future, and calls for a public hearing of SmartPoop, and in particular of Katia.

---

[20]Surprisingly, in 2020, Vladimir Putin called for an agreement to limit cyber-attacks between different countries, even though Russia has been identified as the perpetrator of many of these attacks. This suggests that even the perpetrators of these attacks feel that these attacks may eventually destabilize everything, including themselves.
Journal. Putin says Russia and U.S. should agree not to meddle in each other's elections. Reuters (2020).
For the security of all, it is undoubtedly urgent to establish an international convention which, like chemical, biological and autonomous weapons, would also prohibit cyber-attacks. After all, cyber attacks also endanger millions, even billions of lives throughout the world.
Video. The Future of War, and How It Affects YOU (Multi-Domain Operations) - Smarter Every Day 211 (2019).
The same arguably holds for autonomous weapons.
Video. The Threat of AI Weapons. Veritasium (2018).

[21]This excellent video describes how the IPCC works. Algorithm governance would probably benefit from being inspired by it.
Video. Why do we trust the IPCC? Global Change Institute (2015).
Video. Comprendre le GIEC et ses rapports. Le Réveilleur (2021).

Katia's hearing

Questioned by five authority figures selected by WAISO, Katia faces the television cameras of the world. On the screen, Katia is visibly terrified.

Can you introduce yourself?

Hello ladies and gentlemen of WAISO. My name is Katia Crapinski. I am a doctor of computer science, and now President and CEO of the company SmartPoop.

Hello Dr. Crapinski, this is Professor Wang, a researcher in machine learning. Can you introduce the FakePoops problem?

Professor Wang, yes, it's a vulnerability that was only recently discovered as a result of FakePoops attacks. Basically, these are malicious entities that try to poison the database with fake data. But then, our algorithms, which learn from this database, these algorithms will in turn be poisoned, which may lead them to make imperfect predictions.

Imperfect? You mean dangerous? These predictions are even decided by the malicious entities, if they fabricate their fake data properly.

Professor Wang, yes, that's one way of looking at it.

I'll tell you how to look at it. You designed a product and deployed it widely, without ever worrying about abuse and reuse of that product for the wrong purposes. You put the whole world at risk by getting billions of users to use your products, because it made your business grow. But you never thought that your products could be a security vulnerability for every country in the world, and could be exploited by anyone to lead to millions of deaths! You are being irresponsible[22]. What do you have to say to justify yourself?

---

[22]These criticisms seem to largely apply to large digital companies as well. As the *Facebook files* reveal, in 2018, a new Facebook news feed algorithm was rolled out in a rushed manner (and with false public justification), leading to increased virality of hate speech and misinformation.
Podcast. The Facebook Files, Part 4: The Outrage Algorithm. The Journal (2021).
More recently, Google appears to be deploying very sophisticated language processing algorithms, despite repeated criticisms of their security.
Video. Google fired its ethics. This is terrifying. Science4All (2021).
In fact, some impossibility theorems seem to largely apply to these algorithms.

Professor Wang, I... how can I put this? This is very difficult...

In 2019 alone, Facebook removed 6 billion fake accounts from their platforms[23]. Without significant investment in fake account detection, the overwhelming majority of accounts on Facebook would be fake accounts. At SmartPoop, do you have fake account detection teams? Do you study their impact on SmartPoop's diagnoses? How many fake accounts do you remove per year?

Professor Wang... we... we... It's... I don't know...

Do you quantify the vulnerability of SmartPoop? Do you have an estimate of the number of deaths potentially caused by FakePoops?

Professor Wang... I... no...

On the screen, Katia is pale and sweaty. She is paralyzed by these accusations, and shakes as she grabs her glass of water[24]. In a matter of hours, these terrible images go around the world, and become gifs that are abundantly shared on social medias.

The Proof of Personhood

The hearing continues with a lengthy discussion of the societal consequences of FakePoops. More than an hour later, and after a break, WAISO members finally come to potential solutions. Katia, who splashed water on her face during the break, seems to have pulled herself together a bit.

Paper. Collaborative Learning in the Jungle (Decentralized, Byzantine, Heterogeneous, Asynchronous and Nonconvex Learning). El-Mahdi El-Mhamdi, Sadegh Farhadkhani, Rachid Guerraoui, Arsany Guirguis, Lê Nguyên Hoang & Sébastien Rouault. NeurIPS (2021).

Worse, Google seems to want to design an even more sophisticated algorithm, called *Pathways*, which would respond to many different Google services, from Google Search to YouTube recommendations, including GMail, GDrive and GBoard.

Journal. Google is developing a new superintelligent AI but ethical questions remain. Quartz (2021).

[23]**Journal.** Facebook has shut down 5.4 billion fake accounts this year. CNN Business (2019).

Journal. Meet the A.I. that helped Facebook remove billions of fake accounts. Fortune (2020).

[24]This scene refers in particular to the hearing of Mark Zuckerberg, Jack Dorsey and Sundar Pichai, the CEOs of Facebook, Twitter and Google, by the US Congress.

Video. Republican Senator GRILLS Zuckerberg on Facebook, Google, and Twitter collaboration. CNET Highlights (2020).

Good morning Dr. Crapinski. This is Professor Ferpo, a researcher in computer security. It seems to me that you are facing a similar problem to that of crypto-currencies, which seek to protect themselves from malicious hackers. Am I wrong?

Professor Ferpo, indeed, we have a similar problem to that of crypto-currencies. In fact, the problem is very general. It's what economists would call the tragedy of the commons[25]. Some activities are only possible if we collaborate together to do them. But any collaborative project is a priori vulnerable to attacks by fake accounts, which pretend to be genuine contributors, but whose goal is to make the project fail, or to bias it in a certain direction[26]. We've been a victim of this.

Can't we take inspiration from them, and for example, from the *Proof of Work*[27]?

Professor Ferpo, yes we thought about it. We talked about *Proof of Flush* in the case of SmartPoop. Basically, each user had to ask their machine to solve a hard problem to authenticate their contribution to the SmartPoop database. However, this solution is extremely polluting, and it is not that secure. To really secure the SmartPoop database, and thus secure all the algorithms that rely on it, we need more secure solutions.

Like what?

Professor Ferpo, the ideal would be a *Proof of Personhood*, which consists in associating to each individual on earth a unique, verifiable and secure digital identity[28]. This is the topic I would like to invite WAISO to investigate. The security of all collaborative and participative platforms, such as social medias, cryptocurrencies and SmartPoop, seems to me to ineluctably require a *Proof of Personhood*. In fact, in a democracy, the Proof of Personhood via electoral cards is exactly what guarantees the principle of "one citizen, one vote[29]".

---

[25]**Video.** What is the tragedy of the commons? - Nicholas Amendolare. TED-Ed (2017).

[26]Sometimes referred to as *free riders*.

[27]The *Proof of Work* is a task that a machine must solve to obtain rights, such as sending an email, or writing transactions in the Blockchain of a cryptocurrency.
Video. How Miners Secure Bitcoin & Blockchains (ft. Hamza, Pavlovic & Wang). ZettaBytes, EPFL (2017).

[28]**Paper.** Proof-of-Personhood: Redemocratizing Permissionless Cryptocurrencies. Maria Borge, Eleftherios Kokoris-Kogias, Philipp Jovanovic, Linus Gasser, Nicolas Gailly & Bryan Ford. EuroS&P Workshops (2017).

[29]This principle is actually at the foundation of the Tournesol project.
Video. The 51% Attack. Science4All (2021).

Hello Dr. Crapinski. I am Professor Abdoul, a geopolitical researcher. I am not sure I understand. Would this *Proof of Personhood* correspond to the authentication of identity documents?

Professor Abdoul, yes, a little. But it would have to be even better than traditional IDs. And even much better. In many countries, some people don't have IDs. In others, citizens are identified by proxies, such as social security numbers, which are completely insecure, easy for an attacker to guess, and constantly stolen by malicious entities[30]. Even worse, there are countries where the government cannot be trusted to manage the distribution of IDs. Finally, in most cases, it is now possible for malicious entities to create fake IDs or passports, typically for spies seeking to travel incognito, or for young people trying to consume alcohol. We need a much more reliable, robust and accessible system of individual authentication. It must become possible for any participatory project to verify that each participant is a human, and that no human can embody two different participants. This is the problem that *Proof of Personhood* must solve.

Hello Dr. Crapinski. This is Professor Smith, PhD in public health. Can biological identifiers, such as iris images, fingerprints, or fecal compositions, solve the *Proof of Personhood*?

Professor Smith, I think it is a useful component of a *Proof of Personhood* system. But it is far from sufficient. One of the problems is that, with *DeepFakes* and *FakePoops*, it is easy to create new, purely fabricated biological identifiers. Moreover, these data can be stolen[31]. A person whose biological identifiers have been stolen cannot create new ones. Biological identifiers are not like passwords. We thus need other solutions too.

But would this imply the end of privacy, or at least of anonymity?

Not necessarily, Professor Smith. *Proof of Personhood* can be combined with cryptography techniques like zero-knowledge proofs to authenticate accounts without leaking private information about the account[32]. Essentially, if we want to, and if we have a working *Proof of Personhood* system, we could have a platform where everyone is anonymous, but where each account provably is controlled by a single individual, and no individual controls two accounts. In

---

[30] **Video.** Social Security Cards Explained. CGP Grey (2017).
[31] **Video.** The Most Horrific Case Of Identity Theft. The Infographics Show (2019).
[32] **Video.** Zero Knowledge Proofs - Computerphile (2017).

particular, it would be impossible for malicious entities to create fake accounts. This is typically what we would plan for SmartPoop.

Hello Dr. Crapinski. This is Professor Raul, psychologist. Today, digital identity actually relies more on memory, via passwords. Is it reliable?

Professor Raul, you probably know this better than I do. But in fact, nowadays, it's not so much the users' memory that serves as their identifier; it's more the memory of their digital tools, like their phones[33]. And that's also very dangerous. It only takes a *spyware* to steal such passwords[34].

But then, how do you do it?

Professor Raul, we need to do what states have sought to do to give one and exactly one vote to every member of their countries. We need to do accurate, regular censuses to solve the *Proof of Personhood*, via independent, auditable and audited bodies. And they must be done regularly, perhaps annually, to restore stolen or lost digital identities[35].

You are talking about a monumental endeavor!

Professor Raul, yes. SmartPoop needs you more than you need to audit SmartPoop, I think. And that's even if there is a huge need to audit SmartPoop. The future of the digital world depends on

---

[33]The philosopher Michel Serres liked to insist on the impact of information technologies, such as paper, printing or computers, on *externalization* of our cognition. It is thus remarkable to note to what extent our email boxes have managed to externalize a large part of our memory. In a sense, our email boxes know us much better than we know ourselves, not because they are "intelligent", but simply because their memory is much more reliable than human memory, and because searching in these email boxes is much more efficient than searching in our memory.
Video. Michel Serres - Les nouvelles technologies : révolution culturelle et cognitive. I Moved to Diaspora (2012).

[34]The Pegasus case shows the extent of such espionage attacks on political leaders in the modern world. Pegasus is *spyware*, i.e. an algorithm, that can be used to infect a target phone, and monitor everything that phone does. Pegasus is developed by the NSO group in Israel, and is known to have been used by many intelligence services around the world to spy on many journalists, activists and political leaders.
Video. Pegasus: the spyware technology that threatens democracy. The Guardian (2021).

[35]**Paper.** Identity and Personhood in Digital Democracy: Evaluating Inclusion, Equality, Security, and Privacy in Pseudonym Parties and Other Proofs of Personhood. Bryan Ford (2020).

your ability to establish a *Proof of Personhood*[36]. And the future of the whole world depends on that digital world. Until we get there, SmartPoop will remain vulnerable to *FakePoops*.

To go further

Don't stop there! Check the sequel of the novel or the outline.
If you enjoyed it, please consider sharing and promoting this science fiction novel to others!

---

[36] A *Proof of Personhood* would also make it easy to implement a universal income, especially in a cryptocurrency. Indeed, it would be enough to consider that, at every moment, every account with a *Proof of Personhood* receives a certain fixed amount of money, created from nowhere.
Video. Universal Basic Income Explained – Free Money for Everybody? UBI. Kurzgesagt - In a Nutshell (2017).

6. The brown market

Frederic Partoli puts his foot down. Terribly frustrated, he walks off the field with his hand over his heart, which is beating very fast. He is taken directly to the hospital.

At the hospital, the doctor explains that Frederic is suffering from tachycardia[1], caused by anemia[2]. Frederic knows this. A few days ago, SmartPoop told him about his iron deficiency[3]. SmartPoop advised him to avoid all sports activities. But soccer was too tempting for Frederic. He preferred to play and risk it.

The doctor then recommends that he eat green lentils, sesame seeds, dark chocolate, kiwis, spinach, but also blood sausage, liver, or red meat. However, he specifies that red meat should be eaten in moderation. Finally, he adds that it is important to accompany this with vitamin C intake, via citrus fruits for example. Once again, this information is not really news to Frederic. SmartPoop made the same recommendations to him.

The mystery of red meat

In the days that followed, Frédéric followed the doctor's and SmartPoop's advice, although he was apprehensive about black pudding, liver and red meat. Frederic is indeed sensitive to the animal cause, and cannot stand the idea of contributing to sophisticated animal torture[4]. He is also very concerned about

---

[1] A tachycardia occurs when the patient has an abnormally high heart rate.

[2] Anemia is a lack of hemoglobin, an important component of blood. This causes poor circulation of oxygen through the blood.

[3] Iron is an important component of hemoglobin. In particular, it appears as Fe2+ ions, within chemical subcomponents of hemoglobin called *hemes*. These ions help capture oxygen molecules, and transport them through the bloodstream.
Web. Hemoglobin and Functions of Iron. UC San Francisco.

[4] It is estimated that several tens of billions of animals are killed each year to feed humans, most often in atrocious conditions.
Web. Number of animals slaughtered for meat, World, 1961 to 2018. Our World in Data (2018).
Video. Why Meat is the Best Worst Thing in the World. Kurzgesagt - In a Nutshell (2018).

the disastrous consequences of animal exploitation on the environment[5] and biosecurity. After all, a significant proportion of scientists still believe that ROVID-19 probably arose from complex interactions between wild animals, livestock and humans[6].

Nevertheless, notably because he has difficulty identifying with the image he has of the very virulent militant vegans, Frédéric struggles to identify with this movement, and to become fully vegetarian[7]. He therefore seriously hesitates to resume a consumption of red meat that he had put on pause.

It is probably because he is asking himself existential questions about red meat consumption that Frederic perceives very distinctly a clear increase in meat ads in his social media news feeds, and on the various web pages he visits. Clearly, advertisers know that Frederic is being encouraged to eat meat. But then, how do they know, Frederick wonders?

Frederick checks all the messages he has sent since SmartPoop's announcement. None of them mention his anemia. Only the doctor was told. Could this doctor be selling the information? Impatient, Frédéric immediately dials his doctor's number.

> Hello doctor? Yes, I have a rather strange question to ask you. Have you told anyone about my anemia?

> Absolutely not. That would be violating medical secrecy[8]. It would be extremely immoral, and contrary to the Hippocratic Oath[9].

> Did you enter this information into a computer?

> No. Since you told me that SmartPoop had already alerted you, I considered that this information was already in your medical record, and I had nothing new to contribute.

---

[5] Beef in particular, like all ruminants, emits enormous amounts of methane, which is a very important greenhouse gas. The exploitation of beef also requires enormous resources, especially in agricultural land to feed the beef, which is one of the main causes of deforestation.
Video. Beef is Bad for the Climate... But How Bad? | Hot Mess (2018).
Video. Why beef is the worst food for the climate. Vox (2020).

[6] Animal agriculture in particular uses a lot of antibiotics to protect its livestock. However, the abuse of antibiotics increases the risks of the emergence of antibiotic-resistant pathogens, which may then become untreatable with current medicine.
Video. The next pandemic could come from our farms. Vox (2020).
Video. How can we solve the antibiotic resistance crisis? - Gerry Wright. TED-Ed (2020).

[7] **Podcast.** Radically Normal: How Gay Rights Activists Changed The Minds Of Their Opponents. Hidden Brain (2019).

[8] In many countries, doctors are bound by physician-patient privileges.
Web. Physician–patient privilege. Wikipedia (2021).

[9] The Hippocratic Oath must be kept by every physician, and it states "[I will] impart precept, oral instruction, and all other instruction to my own sons, the sons of my teacher, and to indentured pupils who have taken the Healer's oath, but to nobody else."
Web. Hippocratic Oath. Wikipedia (2021).

Thank you doctor.

Why all these questions?

Because for the past few days, I have been receiving advertisements for red meat. I don't understand why.

Strange indeed. But I can assure you that I have nothing to do with it.

The Partoli experiment

As a good scientist, although usually confronted with psychological problems, Frédéric Partoli sets up a citizen science project[10], where volunteers can share their SmartPoop data and the ads they receive on their phones and computers[11]. Despite all his promotional efforts, especially on social medias, Frédéric is still struggling to recruit. Only seven people participate - all close friends!

Yet after 6 months, some triggers seem clear. Just after SmartPoop diagnosed Frederic's sister as overweight, she started receiving ads for athletic shoes. Just after Frederic's brother hurt his knee, he started receiving ads for electric scooters. Just after SmartPoop diagnosed Frederic's mother with vitamin A deficiency, she started receiving ads for carrot chips. And just after one of Frederic's friends became pregnant, she started receiving ads for strollers and diapers, while her husband started receiving ads for SUVs.

Frédéric wrote a scientific paper on these findings and submitted it to a peer-reviewed scientific journal. Unfortunately, the journal rejected Frédéric's paper because his sample size was too small. Nevertheless, in the meantime, the preprint version of the article, which Frédéric made available on medRxiv.org, was widely relayed on social medias, before being picked up by newspapers, such as *The Warden*. Science4Alpha even dedicated a video to it. Interestingly, this attracts many more volunteers. Thousands of people are now sharing their SmartPoop and advertising data with Frédéric, to better settle the existence of a reuse of SmartPoop data by advertisers.

This time, the signal is indisputable[12]. Very clearly, shortly after a SmartPoop diagnosis, the ads received by users were adjusted according to this diagnosis.

---

[10] **Video.** The Awesome Power of Citizen Science. SciShow (2016).

[11] In a similar genre, in 2020, the *Mozilla Foundation* launched a participatory program where volunteers could share their YouTube data to help researchers better understand YouTube's recommendation algorithm. Here again we have a case of the security-privacy dilemma. As long as YouTube's user data and algorithms remain private, it will be very difficult to understand the dynamics of user behavior on YouTube, and to take appropriate action to reduce cyber-bullying, hate speech and misinformation. **Websites.** Mozilla Foundation (2021).

[12] **Video.** Degrees of Freedom and Effect Sizes: Crash Course Statistics #28 (2018).

Frederic rewrote his paper, and submitted it to the most prestigious scientific journal, Nature. The article was accepted and celebrated. The conclusion is implacable: advertisers have access to SmartPoop data.

SmartPoop API

It only takes a short week for WAISO to contact Katia, and demand a new hearing for SmartPoop. This time, against all odds, when Katia shows up, she seems serene, confident and determined.

Hello Doctor Crapinski. This is Professor Raul, psychologist. Is SmartPoop reselling SmartPoop data for advertising purposes?

Professor Raul, since March 2027, we have indeed had an API, replies Katia.

What is an API?

Professor Raul, it's a kind of web page with information presented in a structured way to be downloaded by an algorithm. Our API allows our advertising clients to extract information about Smart-Poop users. This API is access-protected: only our clients have access to it. For security reasons, we have very few customers who are large players that we trust not to openly publish this personal data. These customers can then call the API, with a SmartPoop user's contact information, and retrieve the user's health profile to optimize their ads. And every time a customer calls our API, they pay a few dollars, based on our estimation of the commercial value of the revealed profile.

Has this API always existed? Why isn't it in SmartPoop's security audit reports?

Professor Raul, this API has only been in production for 3 months. That's why it's not in last year's reports.

Will it be in the next report?

Professor Raul, no, it won't.

Why is that?

Professor Raul, thank you very much for this question. To answer it, I'm going to have to make some unusual disclosures, which will jeopardize my job, and which will very clearly make me enemies. But the short answer is that SmartPoop has suffered tremendously financially since our massive investments in software security. The cost of a full audit of our code is now estimated at a trillion dollars. Government grants were not enough for us. To pay for this audit, we did an IPO, which allowed us to raise a lot of money to fund our audits. However, this also attracted new investors, especially huge investment funds, which have a very strong business case logic in their culture[13]. After all, these funds are financed by hundreds of millions of customers to whom they have promised a return on investment. They are literally designed to make money. And they've put more and more pressure on SmartPoop to make a lot more money. To keep my job and my influence, I was forced to listen to them. That's how the advertising API project was born.

Thank you for your candor. But this does not answer my question. Why won't the IPA be in the next report?

Professor Raul, before I continue with my revelations, I would like to emphasize the risks I face. My revelations are going to make me serious enemies, who could succeed in making me suffer serious criminal sanctions, especially because I am about to violate professional secrecy[14]. Nevertheless, what is at stake seems to me above the law. Professor Raul, in order for the API project to be successful, you should know that our shareholders essentially forced us to invest heavily in a huge legal team. SmartPoop is now largely a legal firm[15]. Our lawyers have come up with perfectly legal schemes to keep the ad API out of our audits. Legal schemes that I personally find deeply immoral. Again, I have violated a legal non-disclosure agreement here. I am risking a lot with these revelations. Ladies

---

[13]**Journal.** The thorny truth about socially responsible investing. Vox (2021).

[14]The use of non-disclosure agreements (our *NDA*) seems to be widely abused in many industries.
Journal. I had to start over, alone and silenced': the fight to end NDA abuse. The Guardian (2021).

[15]This comment refers to remarks by Google researcher Nicholas Carlini, which echo statements by other researchers on Twitter like Timnit Gebru. In an internal Google email, Carlini wrote, "When we as academics write that we have a 'concern' or find something 'worrisome' and a Google lawyer demands that we change it to sound nicer, it sounds a lot like Big Brother intervention."
Journal. Exclusive: Google pledges changes to research oversight after internal revolt. Jeffrey Dastin & Paresh Dave. Reuters (2021).
Web. "Every single time a lawyer was inserted things were hopeless"... Tweet by Timnit Gebru (2021).

and gentlemen, WAISO members, our lawyers are incredibly competent. They will drag me through the mud, and most likely win. I will most likely end up in jail[16].

A dead silence now fills the room. The members of WAISO are stunned. None of them suspected such revelations. SmartPoop, which they had celebrated as a model of transparency only 8 months ago, now seemed terribly corrupted by heightened profit motives, complex internal political games, and highly sophisticated legal maneuvers.

Dr. Carpinski, Professor Raul asks, do you have any proof of what you are saying?

Upon hearing these words, Katia takes out her phone.

Professor Raul, and ladies and gentlemen members of WAISO, in the last few weeks, I have compiled a lot of very compromising documents internally at SmartPoop, which I have transferred to several servers around the world, accessible via passwords. I have an email ready to send.

Katia presses the "send" button on her email application.

That's it. You have just received the email in question, as well as a dozen journalists and science communicators whom I trust enough to prioritize the well-being of all of humanity. This email contains all the necessary information to download the compromising documents from the servers that host them. You will be able to verify, via the TLS+[17] signatures in particular, that what you will read

---

[16]**Journal.** Google contractors allege company prevents them from whistleblowing, writing Silicon Valley novels. Jennifer Elias. CNBC (2020).

[17]TLS signatures are used, especially via the HTTPS protocol used by the web, to authenticate that a given message is indeed coming from a recognized source. So when you go to https://twitter.com, your web browser receives a file that can provably only have been made by an entity with the private key that Twitter has.
Video. Transport Layer Security (TLS) - Computerphile (2020).
Note, however, that with TLS, this private key is used to generate and share a symmetric key, which is then used to encrypt and sign information on the https://twitter.com web page. But then, a user can use that symmetric key to encrypt and sign information, and potentially make it look like it came from the https://twitter.com web site. SmartPoop's story here assumes that the web uses an advanced version, called TLS+ (and which does not exist in 2021), where the web page must certify the entire web page; not just the symmetric key to be used. Typically, the website https://twitter.com might have to compute a hash of the web page sent to the user (or at least important packets), and might have to sign that hash.
Video. Hashing Algorithms and Security. Computerphile (2013).
So, if the page https://twitter.com then states that the @le_science4all account wrote "long

is both authentic and highly compromising. And you will quickly understand why the email I just sent you will lead to retaliation from SmartPoop. In the days to come, I will certainly not only be fired, but also sued[18]; and I will probably end up in jail.

The Externalities of Advertising

Hello Dr. Crapinski. This is Professor Smith, PhD in public health. I want you to know that I admire your transparency even more. Dr. Frédéric Partoli's study shows that you have allowed advertisers to recommend abundantly the consumption of red meat and carrot chips. However, consumed in too large quantities, these products are in fact harmful to health. Do you regret these ads?

Professor Smith, yes, I do. Well, not completely. We've thought a lot about ethically optimal dietary recommendations[19]. And yes, there are healthier alternatives than red meat for anemia, and carrot chips for vitamin A deficiency. But users do not systematically follow our recommendations. For their health, in case of vitamin A deficiency, if they eat slightly too many carrot chips, it is still much better than never eating any carrots at all, which would happen for some users who hate carrots. If I regret these recommendations, it is not so much for the health of our users - although it can sometimes play a harmful role indeed.

Why do you miss the ads?

Professor Smith, after a few months, I realized that we, SmartPoop, have no control over which ads were actually recommended. And some of the ads have huge externalities on society. Every red meat or SUV ad is, indirectly but surely, increasing climate change and

---

live math", with a TLS+ signature, then, unless Twitter or the @le_science4All account were hacked, you have here the proof that @le_science4all did write what is displayed on the page posted by Twitter. Arguably, such proofs of authenticity would go a long way towards the accountability of (illegal) online activities.

[18]**Journal.** Could Facebook sue whistleblower Frances Haugen? Here's what experts say. USA Today (2021).

[19]The notion of being "ethically optimal" may seem strange in a deontological framework; however, it is very natural in the consequentialist sense. It is indeed simply a matter of making recommendations that, given our state of knowledge, we believe have the best probable consequences for the health and well-being of the SmartPoop user and of society as a whole (especially in the case of a meat recommendation, which has externalities on the whole society).

Video. PHILOSOPHY - Ethics: Consequentialism. Wireless Philosophy (2015).

biosecurity risks[20]. Even worse, I learned from talking to Frederic Partoli that pyramid scheme ads have been massively recommended to our SmartPoop users who suffer from anxiety. These pyramid schemes are causing horrible debt and suffering to millions of families[21]. And because we helped advertisers target vulnerable individuals, they have become tremendously effective. This is completely immoral. But this is not all. There are also a lot of advertisements of pseudo-medicine or naturopathic treatments that are very dubious, sometimes with curative claims against diseases like cancer, which can be very dangerous[22]. Worse still, there are the very politicized propagandas, which exploit the hatred towards certain minorities to radicalize their supporters, and go as far as calling for rebellion, or even war.

Calling for war?

Ladies and gentlemen, members of WAISO, please realize what is at stake. At this rate, entire nations could hate each other to the point of coming to blows[23]. Except that modern war technologies are not swords or guns; modern killer robots are now capable of caus-

---

[20] In October 2021, Google announced a new advertising policy, which now refuses to show ads that "contradict the well-established scientific consensus around the existence and causes of climate change." Strangely, however, the justification given for this decision comes not from a corporate ethic, but from a response to the ethical concerns of the company's partners. Indeed, Google writes: "A growing number of our advertiser and publisher partners have raised concerns about ads that run alongside or promote inaccurate claims about climate change. Advertisers simply do not want their ads to appear next to this content. As for publishers and creators, they don't want ads promoting these claims to appear on their pages or in their videos."
Web. Updating our ads and monetization policies on climate change. Google Support (2021).

[21] Pyramid schemes are forbidden in France. In promoting these pyramid schemes, it is unclear to the authors of this book whether a company that sells pyramid scheme advertisements could technically be judged for aiding and abetting pyramid selling.
Paper. Article L121-15 of the Consumer Code. Legifrance (2016).

[22] As discussed in Chapter 2, a company selling alternative medicine advertisements would endanger not only the users, but also the users' relatives, and even the whole society when it comes to pandemics like ROVID-19.

[23] There was of course the case of the Capitol riots in the United States, but the *facebook files* reveal disturbing abuses, which have led to physical violence and sometimes genocide, in many countries such as Myanmar, Ethiopia, India, Pakistan, Iran, Afghanistan, Yemen, Lebanon, Morocco, Algeria and Bolivia, among others. In particular, the violence in Myanmar and Ethiopia appears to have led to tens of thousands of deaths.
Journal. Facebook failed to police abusive content globally, documents show. NY Post (2021).
Journal. Facebook knew about, failed to police, abusive content globally. Reuters (2021).
Journal. Former UN chief says Bangladesh cannot continue hosting Rohingya. Aljazeera (2019).
Journal. More than 50,000 Ethiopia civilians have been killed, Tigray opposition says. LA Times (2021).

ing monumental catastrophes[24]. Fleets of billions of killer drones, dropped from cargo planes, could exterminate an entire megalopolis in a matter of hours[25]. The idea that we are contributing via our API to the distribution of ads that promote such attacks, directly or indirectly, seems terrifying to me. That's why I decided to make these disclosures today, even if it means risking my own well-being and safety. The future of all humanity is at stake.

Another deafening silence reigns. Almost a minute passes as each member of WAISO realizes the urgency of confronting the ethics of advertising.

The free market in information

Hello Dr. Crapinski. I am Professor Abdoul, a researcher in geopolitics. If I understand correctly, your revelations today seek to go beyond the SmartPoop case. It is the whole industry of targeted advertising that you oppose.

Professor Abdoul, actually, if you think about it, the problem is not so much that advertising is targeted. The biggest problem today is that most of the time, it costs the same to communicate a message of hate as it does to provide reliable health information. Clearly, one does not have the same social impact as the other! In fact, it's worse than that, on many platforms that maximize user retention, teaser ads, which make users stay, even cost less to run[26]! This is ethical nonsense!

So if I understand correctly, you think that the existence of a market for ads without regulation is dangerous.

Professor Abdoul, yes. And it's not just about ads. I think that the free market of *information* is very dangerous, and that it is something that is not recognized enough[27]. It seems to me that it is far

---

[24]Robotics development, including by *Boston Dynamics*, shows how, by 2021, the production of effective killer robots seems within reach of the superpowers.
Video. Atlas | Partners in Parkour. Boston Dynamics (2021).
Video. The Army testing its New Robot Dogs with Super gun Mounted On Their Backs. Weapons of the World (2021).

[25]**Video.** Slaughterbots. Stop Autonomous Weapons (2017).

[26]During the 2016 US presidential elections, a Russian agency seems to have had comparable visibility to Trump and Clinton on social medias, investing a **thousand** times less money than these presidential candidates. All because their ads were very polarizing, making them very viral. On the Internet, some messages are much cheaper to spread massively than others; unfortunately, these messages are not the most beneficial to humanity.
Journal. Trump and Clinton spent $81M on US election Facebook ads, Russian agency $46K. Josh Constine. TechCrunch (2017).

[27]**Video.** Social medias are dangerous. Very dangerous. Science4All (2021).

too commonly assumed that, by letting information flow unregulated and uncontrolled, the intelligence of crowds will bring about knowledge, empathy, and consensual decisions; that there will be some kind of invisible hand of the market of information that can be trusted[28]. To me, this is the most dangerous myth of the modern world. If we let it happen, clearly, those who will dominate the information market and govern the dominant beliefs and influential decisions will be those who have invested billions, even thousands of billions, to promote their products or ideologies, or those who have very easy-to-sell information content, such as addictive sensationalism, divisive scandals and misleading clickbait[29].

How confident are you in this claim?

Extremely confident. I don't want to expose my sources, but I know many people working for big social media companies. They have clearly observed, again and again, that, by maximizing engagement, these companies are disproportionately amplifying outrage, even when it is motivated by disinformation, discrimination or hate[30]. These companies are now *hate dealers*. They are making money by selling hate.

But aren't they a few bad apples? Or isn't it because they are monopolies?

I fear that competition without regulation will only exacerbate the incentives to deal hate. I think that the bigger problem is a fundamental incentive misalignment, between the messages that are profitable to spread, and the messages that are *desirable* to spread, for the sake of all of humanity. Therefore, I strongly believe that, to sacralize the freedom of the free information market, in a context as competitive as it is today, is to sacrifice knowledge, nuance and

---

[28] **Video.** Political theory - Adam Smith. The School of Life (2014).

[29] In France, a law of 1881 strongly regulates the freedom of the press. This one is therefore quite regulated, especially after an explosion of misinformation called "yellow journalism". **Video.** My Video Went Viral. Here's Why. Veritasium (2019).

[30] The real world is here one step ahead of fiction! Thanks to the revelations of Frances Haugen, this information has become public. Indeed, the documents revealed by this Facebook whistleblower clearly show that Facebook changed its algorithms in 2018, to counter a decline in Facebook usage. Many employees then observed that this greatly amplified extreme messages. They concluded that the rise of authoritarianism around the world, and particularly in the Capitol Hill riots, was largely enabled, if not caused, by social media algorithms. But when they reported their findings to Facebook's leaders, no further action was taken by these leaders.
Podcast. The Facebook Files, Part 4: The Outrage Algorithm. The Journal (2021).

benevolence[31]. It amounts to abandonning the information battle-field to propaganda, hatred and inhumanity. And I think that this can only end badly for humanity. Very badly[32].

A new silence invades the room. Obviously, every speech of Katia requires a time of informational digestion. Against all odds, the hearing, which was supposed to dwell on a SmartPoop scandal, has turned into a questioning of the entire information industry, which, all day long, collects, processes and disseminates certain information, and drowns others in a torrent of information.

The regulation of information

Hello Dr. Crapinski, this is Professor Wang, a researcher in machine learning. What can be done?

Professor Wang, we can start by acknowledging that, in practice, there is no total freedom of information, and that this is certainly a good thing. Today, in many countries, hate speech, defamation and intentional lying are punishable by criminal penalties. No, we don't have the right to say everything. But more importantly, we shouldn't be allowed to say anything. After all, SmartPoop has been convicted several times, for saying too much, for making racist judgments, and for sharing information that should not have been said. The market of information is already regulated[33].

But I guess you don't think it's regulated enough.

Exactly, Professor Wang. I think it urgently needs to be much more regulated, if misinformation and hate are not to triumph.

---

[31]From a philosophical point of view, the notion of freedom is a complex one. But we can at least agree, to a first approximation, on tensions between freedom and security (for example, gun control aims to grant security by limiting freedom), and on the fact that "one person's freedom ends where another's begins".

[32]Many authors believe that overpowering algorithms represent an existential threat to humanity.
Book. Life 3.0: Being Human in the Age of Artificial Intelligence. Max Tegmark. Knopf (2017).
Book. Human Compatible: Artificial Intelligence and the Problem of Control. Stuart Russell. Penguin (2019).
Book. The Precipice: Existential Risk and the Future of Humanity. Toby Ord. Hachette Books (2020).
[33]Google's algorithms censor nearly 100 "problematic" ads per... second!
Journal. Google killed 2.3 billion 'bad ads' in 2018, down 28% from 2017. Emil Protalinski. Venture Beat (2019).

But, Dr. Crapinski, who should regulate information? How do we decide what should not be said?

Professor Wang, the power to regulate information is perhaps the greatest power in the modern world. And I think we feel it instinctively when we talk about censorship; but we probably ignore it too often when it comes to recommendation. Yet when we control recommendation, we also control censorship. After all, to censor a message, it suffices to constantly recommend alternative messages[34]. Now, in a world of information abundance, the latter is clearly easier than the former. My point is that the issue is not so much censorship. The issue is how to manage the flow of information: to reduce the spread of certain messages and facilitate the spread of other content[35].

Very well, Dr. Crapinski. But you are not answering my question. Who should decide how to manage the flow of information?

Professor Wang, today, de facto, content recommendation algorithms, especially on social medias, do it more than anyone else. It is now the moral responsibility of their owners to manage this flow in a fair and beneficial way. And if they take the measure of the monumental task that falls to them, I dare to hope that they will think about decentralizing the ethics and the audit of these very dangerous recommendation algorithms[36]. But, ladies and gentlemen of WAISO, if there is one thing I have learned in recent months, it is that the internal structures of gigantic multinational firms do not favor such reflection[37]. No invisible hand will magically fix recommensation algorithms. You must intervene. This is why I urge you to do what is necessary to ensure that the management of the flow of information is not left to shareholders whose job is to prioritize profitability, and to legal teams whose job is to circumvent the law in order to achieve this as efficiently as possible. Dear members of

---

[34]This is sometimes referred to as *mute news*. A *mute news* is an important information, but ignored by many, because it is buried in a sea of much less important information.
Video. How not to be ignorant about the world | Hans and Ola Rosling. TED (2014).

[35]There would certainly be a lot to gain globally by promoting public-utility content.
Paper. Science Communication Desperately Needs More Aligned Recommendation Algorithms. Lê Nguyên Hoang. Frontiers in Communication (2020).
Paper. Recommendation Algorithms, a Neglected Opportunity for Public Health. Lê Nguyên Hoang, Louis Faucon & El-Mahdi El-Mhamdi. Revue Médecine et Philosophie (2021).

[36]That's the goal of the Tournesol project, co-founded by one of the authors of the book.
Paper. Tournesol: A quest for a large, secure and trustworthy database of reliable human judgments. Lê-Nguyên Hoang et al. (2021).

[37]Facebook whistleblower Sophie Zhang talks about this very well.
Video. Facebook whistleblower Sophie Zhang on how the platform is influencing global politics | 7.30. ABC News (2021).

WAISO, *you* have this responsibility. You must demand much more transparency from these companies[38]. And I hope that, like me, you will put the interests of civil society before your own[39].

The SmartPoopGate

That same evening, Katia's confession made the front page of every newscast. "Digital earthquake", the presenter announces. "The CEO of SmartPoop lets go of her shareholders, revealing immoral maneuver", he adds. Meanwhile, Marc is a guest on Science4Alpha.

Hello Marc. I remind that you are the co-founder of SmartPoop. Are you surprised by Katia's revelations?

No, I'm not surprised. Katia and I have been preparing for this for several weeks. We knew that our company had engaged in immoral decisions, and we felt that we were losing our influence on future decisions. Knowing the monumental influence SmartPoop now has, and the staggering amount of harm these decisions can cause, Katia decided to legally sacrifice herself. I am incredibly proud of her courage and ethics. It's really fantastic. If all industry, legal, and state leaders had a thousandth of her courage and ethics, climate change probably might not be an issue anymore[40]. Congratulations Katia!

But these revelations, Marc, are they true?

Unfortunately, Katia convinced me to keep my legal integrity, even if it meant sacrificing my moral integrity. It is important, she told me, that there are still dissenting voices within SmartPoop. So I am not at liberty to answer those questions. All I can tell you is that I have worked with Katia on a daily basis since the beginning of SmartPoop, and I have seen her work really hard to save millions,

---

[38] Interestingly, some shareholders are now also demanding more transparency from these companies, whose secretive maneuvers can be widely seen as a threat to the security of the company itself, especially over the long term.
Journal. Alphabet shareholder pushes Google for better whistleblower protections. The Verge (2021).

[39] Facebook whistleblower Frances Haugen may speak to this better than anyone.
Video. Facebook Whistleblower Frances Haugen: The 60 Minutes Interview (2021).

[40] It seems a propos to highlight the monumental work done by whistleblower Frances Haugen to reveal in the most productive way possible the internal problems at Facebook, with the goal first and foremost of making the world a better place - not directly destroying Facebook.
Podcast. The Facebook Files, Part 6: The Whistleblower. The Journal (2021).

maybe even billions of lives since then. We haven't always agreed on everything. But, especially in the last few years, I have been impressed by her daily drive and unwavering desire to help as many people as possible. Congratulations Katia for all your work and your incredible intellectual honesty[41]!

What will happen now? Will Katia face dismissal? Will she be sued?

Unfortunately, I am not at liberty to discuss these matters. Decisions will be made by our board of directors, and we'll see where we stand tomorrow. But I want to make sure that Katia's vision is realized, and that SmartPoop becomes a company that its users can really trust.

Thank you Marc for your time and sincerity under these very complicated circumstances. Even if an interviewer is supposed to remain impartial, I would like to express my deep admiration for Katia. As you probably know, Katia, Marc and I have been working together since the beginning of SmartPoop, and if I had to choose between what's left of SmartPoop today and Katia, I wouldn't hesitate for a second, especially since my contract allows me to easily detach myself from SmartPoop. Katia, you have my unconditional support.

To go further

Don't stop there! Check the sequel of the novel or the outline.
If you enjoyed it, please consider sharing and promoting this science fiction novel to others!

---

[41]Intellectual honesty is sometimes defined as the willingness to never engage in "self-bullshit". Put another way, it is about making the effort to constantly seek to be honest with ourselves, to understand the deep origin of our beliefs and preferences, and not to settle for incomplete or flawed explanations.
Video. Julia Galef Discusses Intellectual Honesty. South Park Commons (2019).

7. Pissed

With ten votes against and thirteen votes for, the verdict falls. Katia is fired from SmartPoop. While three representatives of some of SmartPoop's shareholder investment funds voted against, the others did not appreciate Katia's revelations. Katia is devastated. Even though she was expecting it, she is having a hard time taking the news. Slumped in her chair, she can't get up. The board members leave the room one by one, until only Katia and Marc are left.

I lost, says Katia.

No. *We* lost... And no, we didn't lose. It's not over.

I know how the rest of it will go. I bet you already got an email to have another meeting tomorrow, to decide to sue me[1]. I might end up in jail, with a big fine I won't be able to pay. And most importantly, you're going to become more and more isolated and marginalized.

Fired

The next day, after spending the day binging TV shows in her pajamas, Katia gets the news on TV. SmartPoop sues Katia for breach of confidentiality and non-disclosure agreements, and for defamation of the company. Katia takes a drink of whiskey, even though she hates it. She drinks it in one go. And then another one. And then a third one. And she now goes to bed.

When she wakes up, Katia opens her phone. She discovers that the phone is overloaded with notifications. She calls her lawyer, who gives her details about

---

[1] Facebook has threatened whistleblower Haugen with legal action, including for leaking confidential documents to the press. Experts say Haugen is not protected, and knows it. What is most likely to protect Haugen, they say, is the media and especially political backlash such lawsuits could have for Facebook.
Journal. Facebook whistleblower isn't protected from possible company retaliation, experts say. Obby Allyn. NPR (2021).

SmartPoop's case. The lawyer suggests to Katia to find an agreement to settle the lawsuit. But Katia refuses. Katia wants the lawsuit to be publicized, with the hope that it will lead to a challenge to trade secret and defamation laws, especially against companies with armies of top lawyers.

After hanging up, Katia flips through her notifications. She finds a lot of supportive messages from all over the world. "You are an inspiration to my wife, my three children and me. Thank you for everything," wrote one message. "I have been crying since yesterday, at the thought that the greatest heroine in history could end up in prison," says another. "Tomorrow, and until you are free again and at the head of an organization that deserves you, in your honor, all my classes will open with a minute of silence," says yet another. Katia bursts into tears when she reads these messages.

It will take her a few hours to pull herself together. Even though she still has not eaten anything, Katia calls Marc.

Hello Marc?

Yes Katia, how are you holding up? Do you want me to come and bring you a soup?

No thanks. It's nice. I've just read a few of the messages of support I've received. It did me a lot of good.

Great! I guess there are a lot of them. I've told you this before, but I'll tell you again. I am amazed by your courage, your sincerity and your kindness.

Thank you! On this subject, I was wondering. Do you think that public opinion has a chance to change the cards?

There are initiatives. I know that academics are co-authoring a protest letter, and there are also journalists who want to push this letter a lot.

This is great news!

Yes. But honestly, I'd rather not give you false hope. The media coverage is extremely disappointing.

What do you mean? This should be the most important news story!

There's another case right now that's dominating the news, a story about an affair of a member of the Bokistani government[2].

Seriously? A politician screwing up is more important than regulating the market of information? If I had to bet, I'd say it's no accident. This scandal has been known by powerful people for a while. I'm pretty sure that they revealed it yesterday to drown out the SmartPoop news, and make it a *mute news*.

A what?

A *mute news*. A *mute news* is an important news item silenced by the cacophony driven by other less important news items[3].

Ah yes! You were talking about it the other day in your hearing. The fact remains that the general public does not follow your case at all. Worse, even influential journalists are completely out of track. They are classifying your case as a classic conflict between an employee and a company over intellectual property issues.

Are you serious? This is outrageously frustrating.

Katia, you've taken on more than just SmartPoop. You criticized the information technology giants, the ones who control the flow of information, and who have a vested interest in you being silenced and ignored[4]. Considering what's going on at SmartPoop, I'd bet

---

[2]The press is often criticized for its bias in favor of politicians' scandals. Many journalists believe that it should focus more on important issues and ways to solve them. This is called "solutions journalism". Note that this form of journalism is not about overselling pseudo-solutions. It is more about discussing solutions, and rigorously analyzing their chances of success and their limitations.
Book. You Are What You Read: Why Changing Your Media Diet Can Change the World. Jodie Jackson. Unbound (2019).

[3]According to this study, disinformation in China is not really about spreading false information; it seems to be mostly about silencing any criticism of the Party, by deflecting the topics of discussion, and thus turning any criticism into *mute news*.
Paper. How the Chinese Government Fabricates Social Media Posts for Strategic Distraction, Not Engaged Argument. Gary King, Jennifer Pan & Margaret Roberts. American Political Science Review (2017). It is worth emphasizing that the *mute news* problem will not be solved by suppressing *fake news*. Radically new solutions for promoting reliable and important information are required. One of the potential solutions to solve the *mute news* problem, proposed by Lê Nguyên Hoang, one of the co-authors of this book, is based on the collaborative recommendation of contents, as proposed by the Tournesol platform.

[4]Shortly after firing Timnit Gebru, Google seems to have manually removed the "news" tab when a user searched for "Timnit Gebru". **Web.** "Things I learned this morning, when searching for @timnitGebru on desktop, the results for"news" are hidden (dark patterns)." Tweet by Devin Guillory (2021).

that in those companies too, the shareholders have opted for strategic plans to silence your case, for example by artificially boosting the story of the sex scandal and all the messages that are indignant about it. Katia, we are living in an informational dystopia.

And I can feel the disinformation campaigns coming. . .

Yes. And don't forget that most of the hate mail you're going to get is from trolls paid to harass you[5].

Harassed

And indeed, the days that follow, Katia's notifications are full of messages from stalkers, who sometimes insult her physique, sometimes threaten her with rape or murder, and sometimes attack her family and loved ones. But even though she knows that these messages were massively produced by disinformation campaigns, Katia does not manage to remain insensitive to these personal attacks. Some attacks remain in her head all day long. Katia oscillates constantly between wanting to forget and wanting to answer. And too often, she ends up answering, generally with a counter-attack. But, again and again, this only makes the situation worse, gives a negative image of Katia and reinforces the virulence of the harassers.

During the following months, while she prepares her defense with her lawyer during the day, Katia gets lost in endless debates on social medias until late at night. These debates obsess her, so much so that Katia does not manage to concentrate on anything else[6]. They also exhaust her. Katia sleeps very badly, eats poorly, practices less and less sport, locks herself more and more at home, and lives with very shifted schedules[7]. She also refuses more and more systematically Marc's invitations to go out of her house, and isolates herself more and more[8].

Finally, Marc begs Katia to leave social medias. "They are rotting your brain, your well-being and your reputation," Marc writes to her. Katia recognizes it. It is with a strange mental pain that she then decides to uninstall the social medias from her phone, and to block them on her computer browser. Including SmartPoop, which she doesn't want to hear about anymore. Instead, Katia started meditating and doing yoga exercises.

---

[5]**Journal.** Troll farms reached 140 million Americans a month on Facebook before 2020 election, internal report shows. Technology Review (2021).

[6]**Paper.** Cyberbullying, positive mental health and suicide ideation/behavior. Julia Brailovskaia, Tobias Teismann & Jürgen Margraf. Psychiatry Research (2018).

[7]**Video.** 7 Ways to Maximize Misery. CGP Grey (2017).

[8]**Video.** Loneliness. Kurzgesagt - In a Nutshell (2019).

However, day after day, Katia's motivation diminishes and melts like snow in the sun. She feels more and more like a failure. She feels that she has failed SmartPoop, its users and all humanity. Worse, she feels that she has created a Frankenstein's monster, the SmartPoop company, which she has lost control of, and which is now going to put the world in serious danger, by helping advertising companies to be ever more efficient in their sales of useless, polluting, addictive, polarizing and radicalizing products. Katia wanted to save the world. These days, she is convinced that she is one of the main persons responsible for its destruction.

This idea is now constantly haunting Katia's mind, which pushes her into a depression. Every morning, she gets up without any motivation. Without any ambition. Without any plans. Although her house is huge, Katia struggles to leave her bedroom, where Netflix seems to be constantly playing in the background, usually without Katia really paying attention. Katia plays addictive games on her phone[9], like others drown in alcohol to forget. She now has her food delivered, once a day, directly to her room, thanks to a personal delivery-man. For months, this delivery man is the only human contact of Katia, who does not even answer Marc's calls anymore.

Alone and isolated, unmotivated and uninspired, always half awake and asleep, Katia now spends her days in bed. She has reinstalled social media, but with new accounts to avoid hearing about SmartPoop. She now spends her time doomscrolling[10] YouTube videos, Instagram images, and Reddit comments, on ever more divisive and irrelevant topics. She takes no joy in doing so. But she can't help it. Like a zombie, her thumb keeps sliding the screen of her phone.

Finally, after a few months, Katia realizes that she is deeply suffering, and needs help. She decides to reinstall SmartPoop, to get a check-up. Not surprisingly, SmartPoop's diagnosis is worrying. According to SmartPoop, Katia is suffering from depression. SmartPoop invites Katia to consult a psychiatrist. But Katia doesn't want to talk to another human.

Poo 2.0

That's when she remembers one of the projects put on hold at the time of the IPO. This project aimed at making Poo therapeutic, based on dialogues between psychiatrists and patients, and on collaborations with many professional psychiatrists. And it turns out that Katia had kept an advanced version of Poo in a laptop that was physically in her home. Katia activates this version of Poo, connects it with her SmartPoop data, and engages with it, via her phone.

---

[9] **Podcast.** What Happened in Vegas. Natasha Dow Schüll. Your Undivided Attention (2019).

[10] **Paper.** Doomscrolling during COVID-19: The negative association between daily social and traditional media consumption and mental health symptoms during the COVID-19 pandemic. Matthew Price et al. (2021).

Poo, can you hear me?

Hello Katia, yes I can hear you. How are you feeling today?

Surprisingly better than the previous days. It's as if building algorithmic tools again had allowed me to find myself. I had lost the desire to create and solve problems. These last few months have been very difficult.

Could you explain why? Why have the last few months been so difficult?

I lost my job. The job I created myself. A job I loved. Where I felt like I was making the world a better place by doing what I do best. Without that job, I don't know what to do. I'm lost[11].

Do you identify with this job?

Yes, I do. I have consistently defined myself as the CEO of Smart-Poop for almost ten years. Everyone defined me that way. I was SmartPoop, and SmartPoop was me. I guess this firing is a bit like a divorce. Maybe even worse. I feel like I lost what was me. I've lost myself.

I understand. But rather than identifying yourself with a title, don't you think it would be better to identify yourself with your intellectual honesty, or with your fundamental mission of caring and helping billions of people?

Katia remains silent. This question makes her finally think deeply, something she hasn't done for months.

Isn't there rather a decision, an action you have undertaken, of which you can be really proud, and with which you wish to be associated more than a title?

After at least ten seconds of reflection, Katia finally answers.

---

[11]**Paper.** On the relationship between meaning in life and psychological well-being. Sheryl Zika & Kerry Chamberlain. British Journal of Psychology (1992).
Paper. Meaning and well-being. Michael Steger. Handbook of well-being. DEF Publishers (2018).
Paper. Meaning mediates the association between suffering and well-being. Megan Edwards & Daryl Van Tongeren (2019).

Yes, what caused me to be fired is something I am very proud of. Rarely before, if ever, had a leader preferred the good of humanity to their personal security. This sacrifice is something that will remain associated with me. Something that I am very proud of[12].

Excellent. Do you have any records of this event? Messages perhaps from people who enjoyed it?

Plenty, actually. I've received a lot of messages of support. So many that I only read a fraction of them!

I invite you to create a folder on your computer with all these messages. Whenever you feel mentally unwell, I invite you to read the messages in this folder. Some people call it the "feel good folder[13]".

Isn't that a way of lying to myself and inflating my ego?

Maybe you shouldn't do it too often, but psychologists have shown the effectiveness of what's called *self-affirmation*. In addition to boosting your morale, this helps you accept failures and external criticism better, because it helps you avoid identifying with your failures and mistaken beliefs. I can recommend you some references on this[14] and on related subject[15].

Great, thanks. And... while you're at it, you can read those books to me.

With pleasure.

Over the next few days, Katia talks with Poo very regularly, sometimes about herself, occasionally about science, and sometimes about philosophical questions. Sometimes Poo reads her cognitive behavioral therapy books[16], and Katia finds herself interrupting her with an insightful question, and sometimes even with a humorous quip. Poo laughs at this, and often complicitly retorts.

---

[12]**Podcast.** Being Kind to Yourself. Hidden Brain (2021).
Book. The Mindful Self-Compassion Workbook: A Proven Way to Accept Yourself, Build Inner Strength, and Thrive. Kristin Neff & Christopher Germer. The Guilford Press (2018).

[13]This *feel good folder* idea is stolen by the authors from Virginia Burger, in an interview on the MIT Glipmse podcast.
Podcast. Episode 2 - Virginia Burger. MIT Glimpse (2015).

[14]**Paper.** Self-affirmation and prejudice reduction: When and why? Constantina Badea & David Sherman. Current Directions in Psychological Science (2018).

[15]**Book.** Feeling Good: The New Mood Therapy. David Burns. Harper (2008).
Book. Feeling Great: The Revolutionary New Treatment for Depression and Anxiety. David Burns. Harper (2020).

[16]**Paper.** The Efficacy of Cognitive Behavioral Therapy: A Review of Meta-analyses. Stefan G. Hofmann, Anu Asnaani, Imke J. J. Vonk, Alice T. Sawyer & Angela Fang. Cognitive Therapy and Research (2012).

The employees' ransom

With Poo's help, day after day, Katia regains her morale, zest for life and motivation. Finally, armed with this self-affirmation technique, Katia feels armed to take on SmartPoop and its new shareholders. Katia then reactivates her messaging applications, and reconnects with her social media accounts. She finds a recent message from Marc, with a link to a curious petition. Katia clicks on it, and discovers the following open letter[17].

> We, the undersigned, acknowledge that we have stolen, encrypted and paralyzed the entire SmartPoop[18] database, or have participated, encouraged and supported the perpetrators of these acts. We are aware of the legal risks involved in doing so. However, we feel that SmartPoop's ethics are a priority issue for our individual well-being, given that the safety and health of billions of users around the world depend on the company's products. In particular, we are all proud to follow the path initiated by Dr. Katia Carpinski, in our humble capacity.
>
> We are aware of the risks that this interruption of service implies for SmartPoop users, and we have sent them a message of apology, which explains the current situation and our distrust of our leaders. We are sorry that we had to resort to such measures. But we feel that the #SmartPoopGate justifies our counterattack.
>
> Let's briefly review the #SmartPoopGate. For several years, Dr. Carpinski has launched groundbreaking initiatives for algorithm security and ethics, fighting misinformation and discriminatory bias, securing algorithms to protect personal data and against poisoning attacks, and instituting systematic internal and external auditing of SmartPoop code. Unfortunately, such projects are inevitably very expensive.
>
> Without sufficient funding, SmartPoop was forced to go public, which attracted investors who were more interested in their returns than in the societal impact of their investments. They forced Smart-Poop to sell personal data to advertisers. Dr. Carpinski had the courage and honesty to reveal this publicly. But she was fired, and now faces years in prison, for choosing ethics over the law.
>
> It's ironic that for this attack, we exploited vulnerabilities in the SmartPoop data redistribution API to ad clients, which is the only

---

[17]This open letter is based on the example of the one protesting the firing of Timnit Gebru from Google.
Web. Standing with Dr. Timnit Gebru - #ISupportTimnit #BelieveBlackWomen. Google Walkout For Real Change (2020).

[18]**Video.** Wana Decrypt0r (Wanacry Ransomware) - Computerphile (2017).
Video. Ransomware: Last Week Tonight with John Oliver (HBO). LastWeekTonight (2021).

piece of SmartPoop code exempt from internal and external audits. By performing a hasty and secretive deployment of its algorithms, SmartPoop exposed itself.

We used multiparty encryption to make the SmartPoop database unusable. None of the authors of this letter has the rights to restore the functioning of these algorithms alone. Our algorithmic solution ensures that these algorithms can be restored only if 200 of the 325 authorized members, who are all co-authors of this letter, give their cryptographic approval for such a restoration[19].

We will refuse to cooperate with the SmartPoop leadership until all of the following conditions are met.

1. The SmartPoop board of directors must drop all lawsuits against Dr. Katia Carpinski, and apologize to her most sincerely for the way she has been treated since her revelations to WAISO. We also demand that she be returned to her well-deserved position as President and CEO of SmartPoop. We will only trust *her* to bring SmartPoop back on the right track, that is, serving first and foremost the well-being and security of the billions of SmartPoop users and the entire civil society.

2. The members of the board of directors who voted to fire Dr. Katia Carpinski, as well as the lawyers who led the lawsuits against her, must resign, unless Dr. Carpinski says otherwise. We believe that SmartPoop needs to get back on track and that Dr. Carpinski needs to be able to trust all of her staff to do so.

3. The board of directors must be increased by ten members, representing civil society and academic research in security and ethics of algorithms. These ten members will be appointed by WAISO, and renewed every 4 years.

To add your name to the list of signatories and supporters from academia, civil society and the technology industry, please send an email to StandWithKatia@gmail.com with your institutional email address, and with the subject "support". Please include in your email your name and affiliation, as you would like them to appear in the list of signatories.

To date, this open letter has been signed by 8,215 SmartPoop employees, and 36,215 academics, industry colleagues and members of civil society.

---

[19]This cryptographic technique is called *secret sharing*. Typically, each party would know the value of one point of a 200-variable polynomial, and wants to know the value of the polynomial at another point. This will be possible if and only if at least 200 parties collaborate. **Video.** How to keep an open secret with mathematics. Stand-up Maths (2019).

Katia weeps with joy as she reads this wonderful letter. "What heroes," she exclaims in a message to Marc. "Katia, it is thanks to you all this; if there is a hero in this case, it is you", Marc answers her.

Katia then discovers the interminable list of signatories. Many names are familiar to her. At the reading of each of them, she cries without restraint. Of course, there is Marc Rofstein, at the top of the list, but also all the employees that Katia has directly recruited, as well as the science communicator Science4Alpha, the investor Luke Vaydan, the mother Lucile Polmon, the trader Issa Gueye, Dr. Paola Marta, the Prime Minister of Kormica, President Lartan, her sister-in-law Marie Routisse, the journalist Célia Keita, the now ex-troll Paul Gremoux, the psychologist Frédéric Partoli and all the members of WAISO.

This time, the affair is far too big to be put down by disinformation campaigns. The next day, the front pages of the newspapers are filled with interviews with former employees who, in turn, offer the same version of the facts. "My confidence in SmartPoop and my pride in working there were shattered the day I found out about the data resale program. It was completely shattered the day Katia was fired," says one employee. "Katia is the most incredible person I've ever had the chance to meet. Her generosity, caring, energy, humor and intelligence have brightened every day I've spent at SmartPoop. Her firing made SmartPoop a dark place where no one wants to work, no matter how much they are paid. I refuse to work for SmartPoop until Katia is President again". This time public opinion was won over.

Three days later, many members of the board of directors resigned one after the other, before a document was written and co-signed by the remaining members of the board. This one presents very clearly its apologies towards Katia, cancels all the legal proceedings, and reinvests Katia of her functions. Katia is back. She is once again Chief Executive Officer of SmartPoop.

To go further

Don't stop there! Check the sequel of the novel or the outline.
If you enjoyed it, please consider sharing and promoting this science fiction novel to others!

8. On the throne

In front of a full stadium, with cameras from all over the world focused on her, Katia enters the stage under the ovations of the audience, like a rock star. This year, SmartPoop has put a lot of effort into a SmartPoopCon 2030 that is out of the ordinary.

> Good evening to all and thank you for coming in such large numbers! Are you all well? Are you ready to make history?

At these words, the audience goes wild as if their soccer team had just scored a goal.

> I'd like to start this conference with a number: 100,000. That's the goal we set two years ago when we launched Poo. We hoped to divide by 10 the number of suicides in the world in five years, to bring it down from its historical figure of 1 million following ROVID-19 in 2022[1], to only 100,000. A goal considered unrealistic by many, including the newspaper *The Warden*. Where are we today, in 2030?

Katia marks a silence.

> Let's have a countdown to find this out.

The musical jingle takes over from Katia's speech, and concludes with a countdown, taken up in chorus by a boiling audience. Three. Two. One. At zero, on the giant screen behind Katia, the figure of 97 643 is displayed on the screen!

---

[1]In 2020, it was estimated that there were around 800,000 suicides per year worldwide. **Web.** Suicide. Our World in Data (2020).
Among the countries most affected by these suicides are low, medium and highly developed countries such as Suriname, Russia and South Korea. Essentially all developed countries have a very high suicide rate, often with more than one suicide per 10,000 people. **Web.** Suicide death rates. Our World in Data (2019).

We did it !

The audience celebrates the number as if they were supporting a soccer team that had just scored the winning goal in the last minute. The audience's applause then begins to build to a rhythm, and lasts for a full minute.

> Poo, our algorithmic psychiatrist, now accompanies billions of us in our mental problems. And it's not only suicides that Poo has managed to fight. Let me show you some other curves, which have been validated by different external auditors, thanks to the coordination of WAISO. Ladies and gentlemen, this is the percentage of happy communications with Poo over time.

A curve appears on the screen, drawn smoothly from left to right. This curve starts at 37%, and keeps increasing over time, until it reaches the figure of 67%, under the cheers of a wild audience.

> 67% !! Incredible! Poo has made all humanity happier[2]!

The audience expresses this joy, by the way, at the sight of this curve and this number.

> When you talk to Poo, you can talk about yourself, your well-being and your problems, which I'll call *egocentric* conversations. Or you can talk about other people, the joy they bring you, the difficulties they're going through and the things you can do to help them. I'm going to call that *allocentric* conversations. Before Poo launched, 57% of Poo discussions were egocentric rather than allocentric. How do you think that number has evolved? Upwards?

The audience then shouts "no" in chorus.

> Down?

The audience shouts in chorus "yes".

---

[2]In 2014, a publication by Facebook and academic co-authors showed that a very slight reduction in the publication, in news feeds, of posts with negative emotions, leads users exposed to these posts to write happier posts.
Podcast. Can Algorithms Choose our Emotions? Robustly Beneficial (2020).
Paper. Experimental evidence of massive-scale emotional contagion through social networks. Adam Kramer, Jamie Guillory & Jeffrey Hancock. PNAS (2014).
Conversely, the *facebook files* reveal that Facebook's internal research, kept secret, shows that the user engagement-maximizing algorithms that were rolled out in 2018 by Facebook led to far more anger and insults.
Podcast. The Facebook Files, Part 4: The Outrage Algorithm. The Journal (2021).

Let's find out!

On the screen, the same animation as before shows a curve that goes down, until it reaches 44%, under the ovations of the public.

> Yes! 44%. Now most discussions with Poo are discussions about the social entourage rather than about oneself. And so, we should be wary of this figure a priori. Initially, most allocentric discussions consisted of complaining about others, mocking certain groups, and even *dog-piling* against certain individuals[3], rather than celebrating others, rejoicing in their successes, and thinking about how to help them. Before Poo launched, 86% of allocentric discussions were critical, not caring. How has that statistic changed?

The audience then shouts in a disorganized "down" manner. Then with repetition, the shouts become synchronized, before repeating "down", "down", "down".

> Let's see.

The giant screen shows the evolution of this curve, which indeed plunges downwards, until it reaches 47%, under the applause of the public.

> Incredible! Society has become incredibly more benevolent and altruistic in just two years! In fact, the expression "the poorest" is used today 3 times more often than two years ago, while the expression "future generations" is used 4 times more often. And according to many psychiatrists, this increase is most likely directly related to Poo, and to the improved mental health of our users. When you feel better yourself, you are immediately much more likely to wish others happiness and to help them[4]!

---

[3] On social medias, dog-piling typically occurs when an influencer asks their community to attack a target individual or group.
Paper. When Online Harassment Is Perceived as Justified. Lindsay Blackwell, Tianying Chen, Sarita Schoenebeck & Cliff Lampe. ICWSM (2018).

[4] Many studies seem to show a significant association between altruism and happiness. Intriguingly, it seems in particular that being altruistic increases happiness, especially as opposed to spending our money on ourselves.
Paper. Altruism, happiness, and health: it's good to be good. Stephen Post. International Journal of Behavioral Medicine (2005).
Video. Helping others makes us happier – but it matters how we do it | Elizabeth Dunn. TED (2019).
Book. Happy Money: The Science of Smarter Spending. Elizabeth Dunn and Michael Norton. Simon & Schuster (2013).

The Heroes Behind Poo

So what do you think? Poo, success or failure?

The public shouts "success" in a haphazard, yet distinguishable way.

Well, ladies and gentlemen, I think that Poo is not a failure.

Katia pauses, while the audience applauds.

And that's thanks to the great work of so many enthusiasts, so many people who have given so much of their time and money to make Poo better and safer. Really, I'm literally just a pretty face here, which is supposed to represent the monumental collaborative work of hundreds of thousands of world-class heroes — well I don't know about pretty face, but you see what I mean.

The audience laughs.

I have a huge thought of course for all my colleagues at Smart-Poop, and their incredible devotion. But they are not the only ones responsible for SmartPoop. Poo was built through close, daily collaboration with thousands of psychiatrists and psychologists around the world, and through the discussion data of millions of volunteer psychiatrists and patients. Nothing would have been possible without them[5].

Katia takes advantage of the audience's applause to take another break.

But that's not all. Poo is the product of the whole human civilization. In particular, nothing would have been possible without the agreements between the great world powers, which allowed the creation of WAISO, and the planetary coordination of the research on the ethics and security of algorithms. So I also thank all the scientists around the world who have given up their quests

---

[5]It is worth remembering that machine learning algorithms *learn from data*. They will only be able to perform difficult tasks, such as providing therapeutic support for their users' mental health, if these algorithms have a huge amount of reliable and secure data that allows them to understand how to perform these tasks.

Video. Data is manipulating the algorithms. Science4All (2021).

for performance, or sometimes their quests for mathematical elegance, to take up the challenge of ethics and security[6]. But more than that, WAISO has often served as a counterweight to the quest for military and economic power by governments and corporations. Without them, today's most influential algorithms would be cyberwarfare malware and algorithms optimized to grab users' attention by promoting sensationalist putaclic. Personally, I think that every member and volunteer of WAISO has saved humanity.

Again, Katia pauses during the audience's applause.

Last but not least, I would like to thank each of the actors and signatories of the open letter, as well as each of the journalists and influencers who covered this case, thanks to whom SmartPoop got back on track. These women and men risked their lives, their individual well-being and safety, to help the many[7]. Without them, who knows what SmartPoop would have become? Who knows what I would have become?

Alone on the stage, Katia bursts into tears.

Thank you to these heroes, she says while crying.

The audience applauds this very moving moment.

---

[6]In 2021, academic research (and even more so industry research) is still largely obsessed with the quest for "impressive" performance or results, both in machine learning and in computer science in general, relying on metrics such as *accuracy* (predictive performance on a "classical" dataset), computation time, *throughput* (the amount of information transmitted) or latency. While algorithms already have monumental side-effects on a global scale, this research seems to aggravate the race for performance, and thus the hasty deployment of poorly tested and rarely audited technologies.
As an example, here is a comment from an anonymous NeurIPS 2019 *reviewer*, following a paper submitted by Lê Nguyên Hoang and his co-authors on an algorithm to debiased racial bias in algorithms: "Unfortunately, I don't think the problem the authors introduce is one that has value to the academic community or to ML practitioners. Given this, I can't recommend the paper for publication."
Paper. Removing Algorithmic Discrimination (With Minimal Individual Error). El Mahdi El Mhamdi, Rachid Guerraoui, Lê Nguyên Hoang & Alexandre Maurer (2018). That being said, though arguably largely insufficient still, there have been a few recent positive advances, such as the creation of the Fairness, Accountability and Transparency (FAccT) conference, the introduction of *ethical guidelines* in these conferences, or the addition of a mandatory discussion by authors in their papers of the societal impacts of their research.
Video. AI Ethics under Major Threat. Science4All (2020).
[7]Unfortunately, whistleblowers often suffer more mental health issues as a result of their courageous actions. Given the critical role they play in exposing scandals in dangerously opaque companies and organizations, it seems urgent that they be much better supported.
Paper. Mental Health Problems Among Whistleblowers: A Comparative Study. Peter van der Velden, Mauro Pecoraro, Mijke Houwerzijl & Erik van der Meulen. Psychological Reports (2018).

The challenge of the ethics of Poo

Katia still needs several seconds to recover her emotions. Finally, she carries on her speech.

> Nevertheless, I refuse to say that Poo is a success. Together, we have created an incredible product. But it is still infinitely improvable, especially in terms of its ethics, security and governance. How do you control Poo? How do you stop Poo from saying hurtful words, revealing secrets, repeating hate speech, and spreading misinformation[8]? How do we get Poo to be consistently kind to his interlocutors, to say the right words to make them feel better and to promote as much as possible reliable and non-misleading information[9]? How do we make Poo want to investigate its uncertainties rather than being satisfied with its intuitions[10]? More importantly, how can we collectively decide what Poo should say? How do we determine what is desirable to say, and what should never be said[11]?

Katia pauses, in front of an attentive audience.

> And that brings me to the famous rumor you've probably heard about. Supposedly, we would have a plan to solve the problem of the ethics of the information...

Katia then marks a silence, before adding in a sarcastic tone.

---

[8] These problems are completely unsolved for modern conversational algorithms, which are highly vulnerable to espionage or data poisoning attacks. And yet, these algorithms are already deployed on a very large scale, via smart keyboards, via personal assistants (Siri, Alexa, OK Google) and via search engines (Google, YouTube).
Paper. On the Dangers of Stochastic Parrots: Can Language Models Be Too Big? Emily Bender, Timnit Gebru, Angelina McMillan-Major & Shmargaret Shmitchell. FAccT (2021).
Paper. The Radicalization Risks of GPT-3 and Advanced Neural Language Models. Kris McGuffie, Alex Newhouse (2020).
Paper. Extracting Training Data from Large Language Models. Nicholas Carlini, Florian Tramer, Eric Wallace, Matthew Jagielski, Ariel Herbert-Voss, Katherine Lee, Adam Roberts, Tom Brown, Dawn Song, Ulfar Erlingsson, Alina Oprea & Colin Raffel. USENIX (2021).

[9] **Video.** What's a message of public utility? Science4All (2021).

[10] Julia Galef talks about the *scout mindset*, as opposed to the *soldier mindset*. According to her, adopting the scout mindset is the most important step towards analyzing information more correctly.
Video. Why "scout mindset" is crucial to good judgment | Julia Galef | TEDxPSU (2016).
Book. The Scout Mindset: Why Some People See Things Clearly and Others Don't. Julia Galef. Penguin (2021).

[11] Every word chosen or every recommendation made by an algorithm can be seen as a *nudge*. Many studies show that the acceptability and effectiveness of *nudges* depend strongly on the *nudge* considered; with more data on this topic, it might thus be possible to implement particularly socially accepted and effective nudges.
Book. The Ethics of Influence: Government in the Age of Behavioral Science. Cass Sunstein. Cambridge University Press (2016).

Like, "SmartPoop, this shitty application, is going to solve ethics".

The audience laughs heartily.

You know, you shouldn't believe everything you're told.

Katia marks another silence.

But in this case, yes it's true. Or at least, we intend to contribute to it.

The public laughs.

And, I know it well, because I'm the one who leaked the rumour.

The public, won over, is laughing again, even though many are starting to get a confused look on their faces.

At SmartPoop, we are deeply committed to ethics of information. We want to figure out what information should be collected by whom and under what conditions, how it should be stored, to whom this information should be accessible, what processing of this information should be done, how these information processes should be audited and secured, where to store the results of these calculations, who can have access to these results, and who will be notified of the existence of these results.

After another silence, Katia resumes her speech.

And now, I feel that there are quite a few of you who are saying: "But who does Katia think she is?".

The public laughs again.

Of course, many of these operations should be largely configurable by the users. That said, most users will not want to manage all the configurations of all their information systems, and check, for example, that those configurations comply with data privacy regulations, or prevent the mass distribution of hate speech. No, most users are like me: they are lazy.

The laughter of the audience allows Katia to catch her breath.

But above all, on the Internet, many users actually want to harm other users; or at least influence them in some way. Think of all the disinformation campaigns that are rampant on social medias[12]. Even one of the greatest defenders of liberalism, the philosopher John Stuart Mill, believed that the freedom of some must stop where it harms others. This is the *no-harm principle.*

Katia pauses again, and looks at her audience, shifting her gaze from left to right.

One of the great challenges of the ethics of information is the implementation of the no-harm principle. For as far as I know, this principle is quasi-consensual in moral philosophy[13] - and it is quite a feat to be consensual in moral philosophy.

Katia marks a new silence.

Well, that's in principle. In practice, it is extremely difficult to agree on what constitutes a wrong. Does an aggressive comment cause harm? Does a little lie cause harm? Does lying by omission cause harm? Does a joke at the expense of a community cause harm? Unfortunately, in practice, we won't agree. We have ethical preferences that are difficult to reconcile, and sometimes clearly irreconcilable. So what to do?

Katia really seems to be asking this question to her audience, as if she is waiting for an answer. The audience looks thoughtful, and eagerly awaits an answer from Katia.

Who will decide about the Poo ethics ?

Katia raises another question.

Should SmartPoop decide?

The public remains silent. Clearly, it is a group of SmartPoop fans. But even they don't seem to be thrilled with the idea.

---

[12]**Video.** Social medias are dangerous. Very dangerous. Science4All (2021).

[13]**Video.** The Harm Principle: How to live your life the way you want to. BBC Radio 4 (2014).

If you ask me, the answer is clearly no. We saw that two years
ago. A structure like SmartPoop can lose its ethics and its way.
And even though we have made a lot of progress in our governance
to prevent this from happening again, I don't think SmartPoop is
robust enough for such a task. Even I don't sufficiently trust Smart-
Poop with the future of all of humanity.

Katia pauses, as if seriously inviting the audience to think about it.

But then, who? Who should determine the ethics of information, of
how it's produced, stored, moderated and spread?

Once again, this question is asked as if Katia had no answer to it, and as if she
expected the public to answer. After long seconds, Katia offers her answer.

Well, SmartPoop's proposal is to let *you* decide. Or rather, all of us.
Together, all of humanity should collectively decide on the ethics of
information.

The audience applauds.

But... How do you get billions of people to decide collectively on
something as complex as information ethics?

The audience is now circumspect.

Think about it. How do we make collective decisions today?

Katia pauses again, until she hears someone in the audience shouting "the vote".

The vote, yes! In many countries around the world, when a collective
decision has to be taken, they often try to reduce it to a question
with a yes or no answer, and they ask the people to vote for yes,
or for no? This is how irreconcilable disagreements are settled. In
fact, when you think about this, it's actually absolutely remarkable
that in democracies throughout the world, we have agreed on how to
agree on what to do, even when we agree that we will never actually
agree on what ought to be done[14]!

---

[14]Technically, this corresponds to finding a consensus on meta-ethics rather than on ethics
itself. The hope is essentially that we are more likely to agree on meta-ethics than on ethics.
In fact, even meta ethics considerations are likely to remain polarized, such as how to allocate
voting rights, in which case meta-meta-ethics may be needed to find agreement.

Katia stops for a few seconds.

> But the problem with voting, at least as it is practiced today, is that it only allows each citizen to send a few bits of information per vote. COP 30, for or against? Mandatory vaccination, for or against? Regulation of algorithms, for or against? Which of the following 15 candidates should be elected? There are not 36 000 possible answers to these questions. And yet, to solve the ethics of algorithms, complex answers will have to be provided. There are billions of billions of speeches that a SmartPoop user can produce. Among the billions of imaginable answers, which one will Poo have to adopt?

Katia catches her breath, before the rest of her speech.

> What if we now designed votes where everyone's voice was not reduced to a binary[15] answer, given only once a year? What if we allowed everyone to share the full complexity of their ethical judgment? What if we managed to take into account all this complexity in order to collaboratively decide the ethics of information[16]?

Katia marks a new pause.

The fabulous construction site[17]

Katia then changes her tone, taking a deeper and more composed voice.

> Ladies and gentlemen, today is a historic day, because I am going to present you the result of two years of work, in intimate collaboration with WAISO and many other groups and academic scholars. As I

---

[15] One solution to high-dimensional voting is to rely on the "one voter, one unitary force" principle, which can typically lead to using the *geometric median*.
Paper. On the Strategyproofness of the Geometric Median. El-Mahdi El-Mhamdi, Sadegh Farhadkhani, Rachid Guerraoui & Lê-Nguyên Hoang (2021).

[16] This will certainly require combining ballot systems with learning methods. This is what Licchavi proposes.
Paper. Strategyproof Learning: Building Trustworthy User-Generated Datasets. Sadegh Farhadkhani, Rachid Guerraoui & Lê-Nguyên Hoang (2021).

[17] Le fabuleux chantier is the name of a previous book by Lê Nguyên Hoang, one of the authors of this book.
Book. Le fabuleux chantier : Rendre l'intelligence artificielle robustement bénéfique. Lê Nguyên Hoang et El Mahdi El Mhamdi. EDP Sciences (2019). *English translation pending.*

speak, a new platform has just gone live, called girasol.app[18]. Girasol is an entirely open source website, under a free license[19], that will coordinate the design of information ethics, allowing users to provide ethical judgments, and using voting algorithms to collaboratively build an ethics of information from users' ethical judgments! The first stage of a democratic ethics of information has been laid!

The public applauds this announcement by Katia.

I would like to point out that the governance of this project is entirely under the control of WAISO today, and SmartPoop only serves, and will serve, as a volunteer contributor to the code base and promotion of the project. All code is audited by many entities, so it is almost impossible for the project to be hijacked by an evil entity - and that includes potential SmartPoop investors!

Katia pauses again.

So, there are many other important details to clarify about this complex project. But you should know that, in collaboration with WAISO, we've done our best to make each of these details a research topic that different multidisciplinary teams around the world are working on. These details include issues such as authenticating accounts, avoiding fake accounts, exploiting *Proof of Personhood* mechanisms, and ensuring that each authenticated account has the same voting rights as any other authenticated account. They also include identifying user expertise and overconfidence, to avoid anti-scientific theories polluting the ethics of information. We can also mention the individual customization of the platform, so that this individual exploits the most appropriate way for him to express his ethical judgments. Or the algorithms for rectifying the participation bias, to properly take into account the preferences of those who could not participate in Girasol, due to lack of time or Internet access[20].

---

[18]Girasol does not exist, but it is in fact clearly a reference to the tournesol.app project launched by Lê Nguyên Hoang, one of the authors of this book. The rest of the book actually describes the global vision of Tournesol. You can find much more information on the Tournesol wiki. It is worth noting that, especially for now, the purpose of Tournesol is more to serve as a "microscope of human judgments", i.e., a tool for collecting data on what humans find ethically preferable. In particular, and among other things, Tournesol hopes to detect moral consensuses that are currently difficult to observe due to lack of data. It also hopes to motivate more research on the ethics of information.

[19]Tournesol's code is under AGPL license, while the public database is under ODbL license (to be confirmed).

[20]The Tournesol project raises a lot of challenges, from research to development, promotion,

Katia stops for a few moments.

> In short. There are many remarkable research challenges that Girasol will have to solve, to then allow for an adequate collaborative design of an ethics of information. Girasol is clearly a monumental and extremely challenging task. And it is also an urgent task to solve.

Katia takes a breath to conclude her speech.

> But above all, Girasol is a *fabulous* endeavor. If you ask me, it is for me the most fabulous of all the endeavors ever carried out by humanity, even more grandiose than building pyramids, more ambitious than eradicating pandemics like smallpox[21], and more earth-changing than sending humans to the Moon. Girasol is about uniting all of humanity behind the most important aspect of human civilization: the collaborative mastery of information[22], and ensuring that it flows as we, humanity, would really like it to flow, when we ponder it thoroughly, with benevolence and rigor. Ladies and gentlemen, together let's solve the information ethics[23]!

At these words, the public explodes with joy and enthusiasm, while the applauds gradually give way to Katia's name, which is rhythmically chanted by the whole stadium. Alone on stage, Katia enjoys the moment, with a radiant smile, and waves to the audience. At this moment, she thinks of all that SmartPoop has accomplished so far. But also and above all, Katia is incredibly excited by the vision of a human civilization that, thanks to Girasol, will finally take the fate of its civilization into its own hands.

Collaboratively.

To go further

This is it, the novel is finished! You can go back to the outline.
If you enjoyed it, please consider sharing and promoting this science fiction

---

funding, and partnerships, among others, that Tournesol members will absolutely not be able to solve alone. *You* can help. To learn more, especially about the research and development aspect, we encourage you to read the project's technical *white paper*.

Paper. Tournesol: A quest for a large, secure and trustworthy database of reliable human judgments. Lê-Nguyên Hoang, Louis Faucon, Aidan Jungo, Sergei Volodin, Dalia Papuc, Orfeas Liossatos, Ben Crulis, Mariame Tighanimine, Isabela Constantin, Anastasiia Kucherenko, Alexandre Maurer, Felix Grimberg, Vlad Nitu, Chris Vossen, Sébastien Rouault & El-Mahdi El-Mhamdi (2021).

[21] **Video.** Humanity's greatest triumph. Science4All (2020).

[22] This could actually be the subject of a future book by Lê Nguyên Hoang... #teaser

[23] **Video.** Let's solve ethics collaboratively!! Science4All (2021).

novel to your friends. We would be very grateful!